W9-BRQ-230

For some strange reason, Romeo made her heart race and her temperature soar. Zoe wanted him gone, far away from her, before she embarrassed herself.

"Come on, Zoe, don't leave me in suspense. I need the 411 on you."

"If you must know, I'm the PR director at Casa Di Moda."

Nodding, he snapped his fingers. "I should have known you worked in the fashion industry," he said, his gaze sliding down her physique. "You're stunning and you have a great sense of style, not to mention a unique, eye-catching look."

Zoe didn't respond, searched the streets once again for a taxicab. Romeo was buttering her up, trying to sweet-talk her because he felt guilty about the accident, but it wasn't going to work. Immune to his charms, she wanted nothing to do with him, and gave him her back.

Undeterred, Romeo stepped forward, moved in so close Zoe could smell his minty-fresh breath. Her mind went blank, and her head spun.

Dear Reader,

One summer evening, while bike riding with my children, a distracted driver struck my five-year-old son with her car. Within minutes, the police and paramedics arrived on the scene and quickly assessed my son. Thankfully, he had no injuries, and the driver apologized profusely for the accident. I used this real-life experience as the opening scene for *Seduced by the Tycoon at Christmas*. From the moment Romeo Morretti and Zoe Smith meet, sparks ignite.

Consumed with guilt, Romeo will do anything to prove to Zoe he's a stand-up guy who made a mistake, but the headstrong PR director won't give him the time of day. To win her over, he pursues her relentlessly. Of course he does. He's a Morretti millionaire; *charming* is his middle name!

I hope you enjoyed reading the eighth book in The Morretti Millionaires series as much as I enjoyed writing it. Thank you for your support and encouragement over the past ten years. I am deeply grateful.

All the best in life and love,

Pamela Yaye

Seduced
BY THE TYCOON AT CHRISTMAS

Pamela Yaye

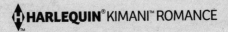

HARLEQUIN® KIMANI™ ROMANCE

If you purchased this book without a cover you should be aware that this book is stolen property. It was reported as "unsold and destroyed" to the publisher, and neither the author nor the publisher has received any payment for this "stripped book."

Recycling programs
for this product may
not exist in your area.

ISBN-13: 978-0-373-86525-3

Seduced by the Tycoon at Christmas

Copyright © 2017 by Pamela Sadadi

All rights reserved. The reproduction, transmission or utilization of this work in whole or in part in any form by any electronic, mechanical or other means, now known or hereinafter invented, including xerography, photocopying and recording, or in any information storage or retrieval system, is forbidden without written permission. For permission please contact Harlequin Kimani, 225 Duncan Mill Road, Toronto, Ontario M3B 3K9, Canada.

This is a work of fiction. Names, characters, places and incidents are either the product of the author's imagination or are used fictitiously, and any resemblance to actual persons, living or dead, business establishments, events or locales is entirely coincidental.

® and TM are trademarks of Harlequin Enterprises Limited or its corporate affiliates. Trademarks indicated with ® are registered in the United States Patent and Trademark Office, the Canadian Intellectual Property Office and in other countries.

For questions and comments about the quality of this book please contact us at CustomerService@Harlequin.com.

Printed in U.S.A.

R0450721278

Pamela Yaye has a bachelor's degree in Christian education. Her love for African American fiction prompted her to pursue a career in writing romance. When she's not working on her latest novel, this busy wife, mother and teacher is watching basketball, cooking or planning her next vacation. Pamela lives in Alberta, Canada, with her gorgeous husband and adorable, but mischievous, son and daughter.

Books by Pamela Yaye

Harlequin Kimani Romance

Promises We Make
Escape to Paradise
Evidence of Desire
Passion by the Book
Designed by Desire
Seduced by the Playboy
Seduced by the CEO
Seduced by the Heir
Seduced by Mr. Right
Heat of Passion
Seduced by the Hero
Seduced by the Mogul
Mocha Pleasures
Seduced by the Bachelor
Seduced by the Tycoon at Christmas

Visit the Author Profile page
at Harlequin.com for more titles.

"We don't meet people by accident.
They are meant to cross our path for a reason."
—Rubyanne from
Read, Love and Learn

Acknowledgments

Special thanks to the incredible staff
at Harlequin Kimani Romance.
You're a hardworking, dedicated bunch,
and I appreciate each and every one of you.

Chapter 1

"Forget it. No way," Romeo Morretti snapped, struggling to control his temper. Scowling though his publicist couldn't see him through the phone, he turned off the stereo system inside his yellow Lamborghini Veneno and took a deep breath. Every morning as he drove to work, Giuseppe Del Piero called to discuss social events in and around Milan. But for the first time in eight years Romeo wished he'd let the call go to voice mail. "I'd sooner run through the city center naked singing 'Ave Maria' than appear on that pathetic gossip show."

"But you love the spotlight," Giuseppe argued. "Always have, always will."

"In light of everything that's happened in recent weeks I think it's best I lie low," he said, rubbing his tired eyes. Working fourteen-hour days, seven days a week, was starting to take its toll on him. Romeo loved his company, Morretti Finance and Investments, and wanted it to achieve even greater success. Hence, he was working around the clock. "I need to focus on my clients, instead of wasting my time doing magazine interviews and TV shows."

"Don't be ridiculous. The press love you, and they're obsessed with your fabulous, jet-setting lifestyle. You're the Italian version of James Bond minus the Secret Service thing. If you shy away from the public now it could hurt your bottom line."

"Life is about more than just money."

Giuseppe scoffed, as if he'd never heard anything more outrageous in his life. "Tell that to my three teenage daughters. The more moolah I give them, the more they want."

Romeo stopped at the intersection and stared out the window. His gaze landed on the corner newsstand, zeroing in on the headline splashed across the front of *Celebrity Patella*. He gripped the steering wheel so hard his veins throbbed.

Scanning the glossy magazine cover, he read the large, bold title—The Morretti Family, Sex, Lies and Secrets Exposed!—and gritted his teeth. For the umpteenth time, he wondered where he'd gone wrong, and cursed the day he'd met Lizabeth Larsen. He'd become acquainted with the lingerie model at a beach in Portugal and it had been lust at first sight.

How could Lizabeth do this to me? Doesn't she have a heart? Romeo couldn't wrap his head around what she'd done. They'd been broken up for over a year, and he hadn't seen or heard from her in months, so why now? Why was she trying to ruin him? She'd given a tell-all interview to the trashy gossip magazine, and now the entire city was buzzing about the salacious story. Lizabeth had shared intimate details about their sex life and had also bad-mouthed his family. Thankfully, his brothers and cousins lived in the States and would probably never see the issue. Romeo, on the other hand, couldn't go anywhere in Milan without people staring at him.

He swallowed hard, but the lump in his throat grew. The negative things Lizabeth had said about his family played in his mind. To his shock, she'd discussed his nephew's fatal pool accident at his brother Emilio's estate, the embezzlement accusations against his cousin Nicco, and his cousin Rafael's baby-mama drama in Washington years earlier. But what hurt Romeo more than anything were the lies she'd told about his deceased mother. He only hoped his grandparents, who lived in a small coastal fishing town, didn't hear about Lizabeth's interview.

"You have to do the show," Giuseppe insisted, raising his voice.

His enthusiasm was palpable, but Romeo didn't share in his publicist's excitement. "I don't have to do shit. It's my decision, not yours, so tell your producer friend at the TV station that I'm not interested in doing a sit-down interview tomorrow. Or any day for that matter."

"Lizabeth made explosive claims about you, and I hear she's planning to publish a tell-all book about your on-again, off-again relationship later as well."

Reeling from the news, Romeo spoke through clenched teeth. "Good for her."

"Want some advice?"

No, he thought, raking a hand through his thick brown hair. *I want you to quit badgering me, and cancel all of my public appearances for the rest of the week. I need a break. I'm feeling run down, and I don't want to end up in the hospital again.* Romeo shuddered to think what would have happened if Giuseppe hadn't found him in his home office that fateful day in August, and pressed his eyes shut to clear his mind. His hospital stay last year had been a huge wake-up call, and Romeo wasn't going to let anyone or anything stand in the way of his health or his happiness. If that meant keeping a low profile, so be it.

"Go on Lifestyle TV, tell your side of the story, then give Lizabeth a million-dollar cash settlement to make her disappear once and for all…"

His eyes wide, he started down at his cell phone, unable to believe what he was hearing. Romeo didn't need this shit. Not today. Every day brought new headaches and problems, and yesterday was no exception. As he was leaving his office for the day, he'd received a phone call from his executive team, and their conversation had left a bitter taste in his mouth. One of his favorite clients, Julio Mario Domínguez, had publicly humiliated Romeo's staff at a business conference in Venice, and his repeated attempts to contact the billionaire businessman had been unsuccessful. The Colombian native was one of his wealthiest and most influential clients, and even though Romeo wanted to keep the entrepreneur happy, he had to stick up for his staff.

"Trust me. I know what I'm doing. It's the only answer. If you don't give her a cash settlement, she'll crucify you and your family in the media."

"A cash settlement? For what? Being mean and vindictive? No way. It's not going to happen." It was only seven o'clock in the morning, but his day was going from bad to worse. Talking to Giuseppe, a jovial character with a boisterous laugh, usually put Romeo in a good mood. Not today. His publicist wanted him to go on TV and dish the dirt about his family, and if that wasn't bad enough, he wanted him to pay Lizabeth off. Hell. To. The. No.

The light turned green, and Romeo stepped on the gas pedal, speeding down the street as if he were on a racetrack. He couldn't believe this was happening—again. Not after everything he'd done for Lizabeth over the years. During their tumultuous, drama-filled relationship, he'd showered her with designer clothes, Cartier jewelry, luxury cars and world-class trips, and how did she replay him? By dragging his name through the mud. Through friends, he'd learned of her bitter quest for revenge, and if Romeo didn't respect her ailing father he'd sue her. "I've given Lizabeth enough money to last a lifetime. I'm not giving her another dime."

An awkward silence infected the phone line. Romeo knew Giuseppe was upset, but he had to do what was right for him, not his publicist. A clean, refreshing scent wafted through the open window, and Romeo took a deep breath. The sun was shining, and the sky was a radiant shade of blue, but the balmy November temperature wasn't enough to brighten his mood. He was so angry about Lizabeth's interview his entire body was tense, and he decided a mid-day workout was in order. At lunch, instead of going to his favorite restaurant with his executive team, he'd use the speed bag in the office gym. Then he'd have a Cuban cigar. He hadn't smoked since he was discharged from the hospital last year, but he was having the day from hell, and a stogie was the perfect antidote for his stress.

"You're the boss," Giuseppe said. "Like you always say, there's no such thing as bad press. We'll find a way to spin the story to your advantage, and you'll come out on top."

I was wrong. There is *such a thing as bad press*, Romeo thought with a heavy heart. This was a nightmare. He'd never been more humiliated in his life, and he hated the cruel, spiteful things his ex-fiancée had said about the people he loved most. Thinking about the lies Lizabeth had told the magazine about him, Romeo decided to call Markos later for legal advice.

A smile curled the corners of his lips. Two weeks ago, he'd traveled to Los Angeles to be the best man at his brother's wedding. It still blew his mind that Markos had tied the knot. Years ago, Markos was a workaholic, determined to be the most successful attorney in the state of California, but program director for a non-profit organization, Tatiyana Washington had captured his heart, and now they were husband and wife.

Giuseppe yapped on and on about creative and innovative ways to increase Romeo's online presence, but Romeo's mind wandered. A year ago, the buzz about his company had reached an all-time high. Thanks to his team, his carefully cultivated image had not only added to his insane popularity in Italy, it attracted women like a sale sign in a boutique window. In the hopes of meeting him, socialites and heiresses had flocked to his office in droves, and once there, he had convinced them to invest with his company. A favorite of gossip bloggers, there was a time when Romeo enjoyed the spotlight. The more brazen he was, the more the public seemed to love him, especially the opposite sex.

Slowing down to allow a jaywalker to cross the street, he reflected on the highs and lows of his life in Milan. He'd done it all—partied too hard, drunk too much and spent money recklessly—but after his hospital stay he'd turned over a new leaf. Quit drinking, smoking cigars and eating like a college frat boy. At thirty-two, hooking up with a different woman every night of the week had lost its appeal, and although he had a life most men would kill for, Romeo felt empty inside, lonely now that his closest friends had wives and children. One by one, his brothers and cousins had found love, and they were all ridiculously happy. Romeo wondered if he was missing out on something. Everyone around him was moving forward, and he was stuck in neutral. For months, he'd been playing it safe, doing everything right and following his doctor's orders, but Christmas was right around the corner and he wanted to enjoy the holidays without stressing out about his health. Or his bitter ex-fiancée.

"Handle it, Giuseppe. I don't want this story hanging over my head during the holidays. Make it go away, *now*."

"*Nessun problema.* Leave everything to me. I know just what to do."

"You better," he said in a stern voice. "Or you're fired."

Giuseppe chuckled. "You wouldn't survive a day without me, and you know it."

A grin overwhelmed his mouth. It was true. Giuseppe wasn't just his publicist, he was also a confidante and a trusted friend. If not for Giuseppe, Romeo wouldn't be alive. "Are you on your way to the office or are you having breakfast with Bellisa again?"

"Bellisa *is* my breakfast," he said with a throaty laugh. "I'll give you a ring in the afternoon, but promise me you'll give some thought to what I said about Lizabeth."

"There's nothing to think about." Switching lanes, Romeo punched the gas. "I'm not giving her a damn thing."

"A million euros is chump change to you."

"Dammit, Giuseppe, it's not about the money."

Making a right turn, Romeo heard something hit the passenger-side door and slammed on the brakes. Frowning, he peered in the rearview mirror. His heart stopped. His cell phone fell from his hands and dropped to his feet. Fearing the worst, Romeo took off his seat belt, threw open his car door and ran around the trunk.

Romeo surveyed the scene. A purple mountain bike lay in a tangled heap on the road along with the contents of a handbag. A woman of Caribbean descent with caramel-brown skin, delicate facial features and waist-length black braids sat on the sidewalk, shaking uncontrollably. Filled with concern, he moved toward her, speaking in a quiet tone of voice.

"Miss, are you okay? Are you hurt?"

Romeo tried to help her to her feet, but she pushed his hands away. Standing, she straightened her short sleeveless dress and brushed the dirt off the hem. Watching her every move, he admired everything about her—her almond-shaped eyes, the beauty mark above her lips, the diamond hoop earrings that grazed her shoulders and her womanly physique. He guessed she was in her early twenties, around the same age as his kid sister, Francesca, and suspected she was an exchange student.

Glaring at him, it was obvious she was pissed, and Romeo didn't blame her. He should have been paying attention to the road instead of arguing with Giuseppe about his ex. He'd messed up, and now because of his mistake the cyclist was staring at him with tears in her eyes.

Romeo swallowed hard. Feeling like a specimen under a microspore, his throat dried, and sweat drenched his suit jacket. If looks could kill, he'd be dead, and the coroner would be notifying his next of kin. For the first time in Romeo's life he was tongue-tied, in such a state of shock he couldn't speak. And not just because he'd accidentally struck a cyclist with his car; he was transfixed by the woman's natural beauty. There weren't a lot of people of color in Milan, and she was such a knockout that Romeo couldn't stop staring at her. Her full, sensuous lips and her Lord-have-mercy curves were captivating, instantly seizing his attention.

Romeo was intrigued by her, wanted to know her story. Where was she from? And most importantly, was she single? The woman was off-the-charts hot, and if they'd met under different circumstances he definitely would have asked her out. But since Romeo didn't want her to think he was an insensitive jerk, he quit lusting and wore an apologetic smile. "Miss, I feel horrible about what happened."

Drawn to her, he stepped forward, eager to make amends for what he'd done. Romeo felt like an ass. Guilt-ridden, he opened his mouth to apologize again, but her strident voice filled the air.

"Are you blind?" she shouted. "You could have killed me with your stupid sports car!"

A crowd of curious onlookers had gathered around them, and Romeo wished everyone—except the dark-skinned beauty with the American accent—would disappear. Well-traveled, with vacation homes and real estate properties all across the United States, he guessed she was visiting from New York and wondered how long she'd be in Milan.

The woman gestured to the road, an incredulous expression on her flawless oval face. "I had the right of way, but you turned *right* into me. What's wrong with you? You couldn't wait ten seconds for me to cross the street?"

"Miss, I'm sorry. I didn't see you—"

"Of course you didn't see me," she shot back. "You were too busy on your cell phone."

"You're right," Romeo conceded. "I should have been paying more attention to the road."

"Jerk," she mumbled, shaking her head in disgust. "You should lose your license."

Gasps and whispers ripped through the well-dressed Milanese crowd. A camera flashed in Romeo's face, then another one, and he knew it was just a matter of time before everyone in the city knew about his morning traffic accident. *Great*, he thought, shoving his hands into the pockets of his black, suit pants. *That's all I need. More bad press.*

Horns blared, and pedestrians complained as they maneuvered their way around the accident scene. An irate driver in a gleaming white Porsche stuck his head out the window and yelled in Italian about the traffic jam.

Romeo's car was blocking the intersection, but the street was so narrow that there was nowhere for him to move it. "The accident was my fault, and I take full responsibility for it," he said, hoping to defuse the situation. "I'll pay to replace your bike, your dress and all of the contents in your purse as well—"

"How benevolent of you, Mr. Morretti, but I don't want anything from you."

His mouth fell open, and seconds passed before he spoke. "You know who I am?"

"Of course I know who you are. I haven't been living under a rock the last two years."

"You live here? In Milan?" Romeo asked. "Where?"

A bearded man holding a leather satchel made his way through the crowd. "My name is Lucan Bianchi and I'm an emergency room doctor at Milan General Hospital," he explained, addressing the cyclist. "Is it okay if I check you out while we wait for the paramedics to arrive?"

Nodding, the woman allowed the doctor to lead her over to a wooden bench under a cluster of lush green trees, and she took seat. To Romeo's relief, most of the spectators put their cell phones away and moved on. He heard sirens in the distance, knew the police were on their way to the scene and considered calling Giuseppe back. This was bad. Worse than the stories about him in the tabloids. He'd screwed up and needed his public relations director to work his magic again.

Romeo shook his head. No. He'd handle it. He'd take responsibility for his actions and would deal with the consequences, whatever they may be. But a chilling thought came to mind, and a shudder ripped through his body. What if there was footage of his accident? If the police brought charges against him, would his reputation suffer? Would his billionaire clients take their investments elsewhere? His pulse drummed in his ears, deafening him. Romeo could see the headlines now: Woman Struck by Morretti Millionaire! Wealthy Businessman Charged with Careless Driving! Jail Time for Bad-Boy Tycoon!

"Zoe, where are you visiting from?"

The sound of the doctor's voice interrupted Romeo's thoughts. Eager to learn more about the cyclist, he listened closely to the conversation she was having with the physician. It was a challenge, but Romeo blocked out all the noises on the busy street and committed everything about her to memory. Her name was Zoe Smith; she'd lived in Milan for two years and was the PR director for the fashion house Casa Di Moda. He'd never heard of the company before, but made a mental note to Google it when he returned to his car.

Trying to appear casual, he moved closer to the bench and listened in. Romeo was used to meeting beautiful females and had no shortage of admirers, but this was the first—and only—time in his life a woman had left him flustered, desperate to be in her presence. He couldn't take his eyes off of her and wished he could trade places with the doctor. The physician had the pleasure of touching her, and as Romeo stared at the dark-skinned beauty, all he could think about was kissing her. Undressing her. Making love to her at his villa. And he would. But first, Romeo had to save his neck.

Chapter 2

Zoe Smith stood on the corner of the traffic-congested road, watching the female paramedics fawn all over Romeo Morretti, and rolled her eyes. They were flirting with him, acting as if they were socializing at a cocktail party rather than at the scene of a traffic accident. Their behavior was annoying her. They were flipping their hair, batting their eyelashes, laughing outrageously every five seconds. Why were they showering him with attention? Why weren't they assessing her—the victim? Wasn't that their job? To help her?

Romeo caught her staring at him, and her heart stopped. Zoe wanted to look away, but his gaze held her in its seductive grip. Even though she was a mature, thirty-two-year-old woman, she couldn't muster the strength to break free. The media—and every female in the city—loved the brazen playboy, and although she'd seen numerous pictures of him in the tabloids, Zoe still gave him the once-over. Dressed in a tailored suit, it was easy for her to see why socialites, actresses and pop stars threw themselves at him on a daily basis. He was eye candy. The kind of man women fantasized about, men idolized and children adored. Romeo was twenty feet away from her, but he still made her breathless. Light-headed. It was more than just his ridiculous sex appeal and his dark, soulful features; his calm, cool demeanor drew her in. He was trouble though, no doubt about it. Thoughts she had no business having about Romeo filled her mind, and she couldn't escape them.

Giving her head a shake, Zoe tore her gaze away from his handsome face. She hadn't traveled all the way to Milan to get played by a cocky bachelor with a reputation with the ladies. She'd read the stories in the tabloids, and now that she'd met Romeo Morretti for herself, Zoe knew the gossip was true. According to published reports, he was used to getting his way in the boardroom *and* the bedroom, but she wasn't going to give him the time of day. She was actively searching for Mr. Right, not a bad-boy businessman who reeked of arrogance.

Zoe glanced at her wristwatch, saw that it was eight thirty and felt a rush of panic. The staff meeting started in thirty minutes, and since she didn't want to miss Aurora's announcement, she had to hurry. Her office was only ten minutes away, and once the police finished their investigation, she'd be on her way. Her colleagues at Casa Di Moda were convinced they were receiving Christmas bonuses today, and the news was music to her ears.

For the first time that morning, Zoe smiled. Drowning in debt, she planned to use the money to pay off her bills and buy a plane ticket to New York so she could spend the holidays with her family. Milan was expensive, and it was impossible for her to save money when she had to network every night of the week. Not that Zoe was complaining. She attended red-carpet events, charity galas and award shows, and mingled with the most important people in the fashion industry. In two short years, she'd developed strong relationships with magazine editors, beauty bloggers and supermodels, and her boss was thrilled with the progress she'd made. Best of all, she loved the energy and environment at Casa Di Moda, and hoped to work at the up-and-coming fashion house for many years to come.

"Ms. Smith, would you like to add anything else to your statement?"

Surfacing from her thoughts, Zoe shook her head and faced the police officer with the heavy accent and wiry black hair. "What happens now?" she asked. "Are you going to charge Mr. Morretti with distracted driving?"

The officer closed his notebook and tucked it into his front pocket. "No."

"Why not? He was yapping on his cell phone and driving recklessly when the accident occurred. If that isn't the definition of distracted driving, I don't know what is."

"Witnesses said Mr. Morretti had the right of way when you slammed into his car."

"Yeah, right. And I was an astronaut in a past life," she quipped.

The officer frowned. "Why would the witnesses lie? Furthermore, I interviewed everyone in the café across the street and the staff said the same thing. *You* crossed illegally."

Stumped, Zoe closed her mouth. *Am I at fault? Did I cause the accident?* She tried to remember what happened, to visualize the scene in her mind's eye, but her brain was foggy. Last night, she'd stayed up late working on the December events calendar, and Zoe was so tired, she'd dozed off at the kitchen table while reading the morning newspaper.

Her gaze landed on her mountain bike, lying in pieces on the cobblestoned road, and her shoulders sagged. Milan was flat, with no hills or valleys, and biking around the city was not only fun and economical, it was a great way for her to learn her way around. It had been a gift from her colleague, Jiovanni Costa, and Zoe had fond memories of them cycling through the countryside, talking, laughing and cracking jokes. The associate designer was the brother she'd never had, and if not for his friendship she never would've survived her first month in Milan.

"Am I free to go?" Zoe asked, addressing the police officers.

"You should go to the hospital to get checked out," the emergency room doctor advised, pushing his rimless eyeglasses up the bridge of his nose. "I think it's for the best."

The police officer with the crooked teeth nodded his head. "I agree."

Zoe was annoyed, but she didn't argue with the three men crowded around her on the wooden bench. It wasn't their fault Romeo Morretti had ruined her morning commute, and although she was tired of the doctor pressuring her to go to the hospital, she hid her frustration. "Thanks, but no thanks," Zoe said, rising to her feet. Pain coursed through her right ankle, but she ignored the discomfort. "I'm good."

Worry lines wrinkled the doctor's forehead. "But you're favoring your right side."

He was right; she was. Dodging his gaze, Zoe stared down at her wedge sandals. Her shin was sore and her legs ached, but since it was nothing a warm bath and a glass of Chianti couldn't cure, Zoe dismissed his concerns with a wave of her hand. "I'm fine. I don't need to go the hospital. I need to go to work, and if I don't leave now, I'll be late."

The men shared a worried look, and Zoe wondered if the police had the authority to take her to the hospital against her will. Anxious to get to the office, she crouched down on the road, grabbed her broken handbag and stuffed her personal items back inside. Her cell phone and her tablet were both cracked, and her makeup case was caked in mud. Pausing to look at the family pictures that had fallen out of her journal, her vision blurred. As she'd collided with Romeo Morretti's car, images of her parents and her younger sister had flashed before her eyes. If her cell phone weren't broken, she'd call them right now just to hear their voices. It was hard being away from her close-knit Trinidadian family, but Zoe loved living and working in Milan and wanted to help make Casa Di Moda a household name.

Standing, Zoe glanced around for a taxi stand. Spotting one across the street in front of a bakery, she swung her purse over her shoulder and gingerly approached the intersection. If she hurried, she could make it to the staff meeting on time, and her boss would never know she'd been an hour late for work. Zoe still couldn't wrap her mind around what had happened. Her bike was destroyed, but she was alive and well, and that was all that mattered.

"Hey! Wait! Where are you going?" the police officer said, raising his voice. "You can't leave your bike on the road all day. Someone could get hurt."

Zoe frowned. What did he expect her to do? Carry it on her back to work? His tone was sharp, implying that his patience was limited. To smooth things over, she apologized for the inconvenience and thanked the officers in Italian for their help.

Everyone on the sidewalk—including Romeo Morretti—gawked at her. No doubt, they were shocked she spoke Italian. Everyone was. Two years ago, while traveling through Europe, she'd fallen in love with Milan, and after a chance meeting with up-and-coming fashion designer Aurora Bordellio at a networking event, she'd landed the public relations director position at Casa Di Moda. Thrilled to be living and working in her favorite city in the world, she'd devoted herself to learning the language, culture and history. Taking night classes at the local university and attending community events were the wisest things she'd ever done. When locals heard her speaking Italian, they instantly warmed up to her and went out of their way to help her.

The light changed, and pedestrians flooded the street. Taking her time, despite all of the people rushing past her, Zoe slowly crossed the intersection. High-rise buildings crowded the skyline, but she could still make out the top of the golden-painted statue on the Duomo and admired its beauty. Described by locals as the Italian Manhattan, Milan was a fast-paced city packed with entrepreneurs, university students, attractive women in the latest designer fashions, and wide-eyed tourists toting cameras and backpacks.

Zoe was tired and her ankle ached, but the sounds and aromas around her were invigorating. Milan had it all—historical buildings and monuments, breathtaking architecture, outstanding restaurants, and a vibrant nightlife—and every day, Zoe found something new to love about the city. Her work visa expired in the new year, and although she missed her friends and family back home, she teared up at the thought of leaving Milan.

"Where are you going?"

Zoe glanced over her shoulder and saw Romeo Morretti standing directly behind her, and gulped. *What does he want?* Her eyes zeroed in on him, taking in every aspect of his six-foot-three frame. He had a full head of curly brown hair and skin that looked smooth to the touch, and his lips were so thick and juicy, thoughts of kissing him overwhelmed her mind. He smelled of shampoo and aftershave; the strong, masculine scent tickled her nose. His piercing gaze and his boyish smile were a lethal combination. Zoe feared if she didn't move, her knees would buckle, and she'd fall headfirst into his arms. Desperate to put some distance between them, she increased her pace, speed walking toward the taxi stand even though her ankle was killing her.

"Zoe, please, wait. Don't run off. I can drive you wherever you need to go."

Her feet slowed. Not because of his generous, unexpected offer, but because of the way he said her name. With tenderness and warmth, as if they were lovers and he was pleading for forgiveness. Deleting the thought from her mind, Zoe knew it was important to keep her guard up and wisely took cover behind the green taxi stand. Her mouth was dry, and her stomach was twisted in knots, but she managed to sound calm. "No, thank you."

"Why not?"

"I've seen you drive, and I don't want to end up in the emergency ward."

The light in his eyes dimmed, and Zoe felt guilty for insulting him. She remembered what the police officers had told her about the accident. According to witnesses, she was to blame, so she had no right to insult Romeo Morretti. Still, he made her nervous, uncomfortable. She wished he'd return to his fancy sports car and leave her alone.

"Where are you going?"

"Work," she said, trying to conceal her frustration. Hot and thirsty, all Zoe could think about was drinking a tall, cold glass of ice water, and hoped Jiovanni had remembered to bring snacks to the staff meeting. "I'm late, and if I don't hustle, my boss will kill me."

"Work? In your condition?" His eyebrows slanted in a frown. "You should go home and rest. I'm sure your boss will understand."

"Has anyone ever told you that you're a pest?"

Romeo gave a hearty chuckle. "No, never."

Damn, even his laugh is sexy, Zoe thought as she wiped her damp palms along the sides of her dress. It wasn't every day she met a man of Romeo Morretti's calibre—someone suave, charming and dapper—and being in his presence had an odd effect on her. Every time their eyes met she felt short of breath, as if she were going to have an asthma attack—but she didn't have asthma. Licking her lips, she searched the street for a cab.

"Zoe, what's the number for Casa Di Moda? I'll call on your behalf."

A shiver tickled her spine. Hearing her name come out of his broad, sensuous mouth warmed her all over. Seconds passed before she could speak, and when Zoe finally reunited with her voice, it sounded foreign to her ears. *What's the matter with me? Why am I acting skittish?* For some strange reason, Romeo made her heart race. Zoe wanted him gone, far away from her, before she embarrassed herself.

"No thanks, I'm good. Don't bother."

"I should have known you worked in the fashion industry," he said, his gaze sliding down her physique. "You're stunning, and you have a great sense of style, not to mention a unique, eye-catching look."

Zoe didn't respond, searched the streets once again for a taxicab. Romeo was buttering her up, trying to sweet-talk her because he felt guilty about the accident, but it wasn't going to work. Immune to his charms, she gave him her back.

Undeterred, Romeo stepped forward, moved in so close, Zoe could smell his minty-fresh breath. Her mind went blank and her senses spun. They were standing side by side now, shoulder to shoulder, and for the second time in minutes, Zoe inhaled sharply.

"You speak Italian very well," Romeo said, his tone filled with awe. "How did you learn the language?"

Doesn't he have somewhere to be? His office? A meeting? On his private jet with a bevy of supermodels? Zoe told herself to be nice and forced a smile on her lips. "I took Italian in high school and throughout university, so I had a good handle on the language before I moved to Milan."

Annoyed that her favorite pair of sunglasses had been destroyed in the accident, she shielded her eyes from the sun with her hands. The sky was a brilliant shade of blue, the breeze was warm, and a delicious scent wafted out of the bakery, eliciting groans from her stomach. Zoe thought of going inside the shop to grab a bite to eat, but decided against it. She was pressed for time, and she feared Romeo Morretti would follow her inside if she did. The last thing she wanted was to be alone with him in a cozy, intimate setting. He made her jittery, and there was no telling what would happen if he touched her again.

"I feel horrible about the accident, and I want to make it up to you."

Zoe didn't answer, hoping that if she stayed quiet, he'd take the hint and go away.

"I'd like to take you out for dinner tonight at Dolce Vita Milan," he said.

His broad smile revealed straight, blinding white teeth and dimples in each cheek. He was a pretty boy who was used to getting his way, and although he wasn't her type,

Zoe had to admit that Romeo was one fine-looking man. A handful, too, according to her favorite blog. Every week, there was a story about him hooking up with an Italian actress or model. Zoe didn't doubt it. He had a devilish expression on his face, as if he was cooking up mischief, and Zoe suspected this was his MO—flash a wink and a smile, then pour on the charm. She made up her mind not to be his next victim. Dubbed *Diavolo Sexy* by the local press, which meant sexy devil in Italian, Romeo could have any woman he wanted, and Zoe didn't doubt that he had.

"Put your number in my phone," he instructed, taking his cell out of his back pocket and offering it to her. "I'll call you this afternoon so we can hook up."

Zoe narrowed her eyes. Hook up? After five minutes of conversation? Boy, bye!

Disgust must have shown on her face, because Romeo wore an apologetic smile and brushed his fingertips against her forearm.

"What is it, *bellissima*? You look upset. Did I say something wrong?"

Beautiful? Overcome by his close proximity, Zoe dodged his sexy, steely stare. *Romeo thinks I'm beautiful?* Goose bumps flooded her skin. Feeling out of sorts, as if a shy, flustered teenager had suddenly inhabited her body, her mouth dried and her heart beat in triple time. "You don't have to buy me dinner. It was an accident, and since the police said I'm to blame, you don't owe me anything."

"I'd still like to take you out tonight. I love being in the presence of smart, accomplished women. I think we'll have a great time together at Dolce Vita Milan."

Swallowing hard, Zoe fingered the gold pendant at her neck. "Thanks, but no thanks," she said, still convinced he was up to something. "We're strangers, and—"

"That's why I want us to have dinner. We'll have a nice

meal, a bottle of your favorite wine, and get to know each other better. Doesn't that sound like fun, Zoe?"

Romeo licked his lips with such finesse her skin tingled. It was a struggle, but Zoe maintained her composure, didn't wither under the intensity of his dark, smoldering gaze.

"I can't. I have a work function to attend."

"I understand. No problem. We can have dinner tomorrow night. Same time and place."

Zoe shook her head. "I have plans with friends."

"Cancel them." Glancing around, he lowered his face to hers and spoke in a quiet voice. "We need to get our stories straight about the accident. I don't want any surprises."

His words didn't register. "I don't understand."

"I think you do, but we can discuss the details tomorrow night at dinner."

A taxicab stopped at the curb, and Zoe sighed in relief. "I have to go."

"Not so fast." Romeo put his hand on the passenger side door, thwarting her escape. "You still haven't given me your cell number. How am I supposed to finalize our plans if I don't know how to reach you?"

Zoe couldn't believe his nerve. *Who does he think he is? My man?* The time for being nice was over. It was time to make herself crystal clear. "We're not having dinner tomorrow night or any other night. Now if you'll excuse me, I have to go."

He looked shell-shocked, like a survivor stumbling off a shipwrecked boat. Zoe suspected a woman had never told him no before. Proud of herself for not falling victim to his charms, she gestured to the door and smiled her thanks when he reluctantly opened it.

"Zoe, please, reconsider meeting with me. I know we can work something out."

"There's nothing to reconsider."

To her surprise, Romeo reached into his pocket, took out his wallet and handed the driver several dollar bills. Lowering his head through the open window, his cologne engulfing the compact car, he spoke to the driver in Italian.

His words made her heart smile. *Take this beautiful woman anywhere she wants to go.* Zoe couldn't deny it, the man had a way with words. Romeo straightened to his full height, and watching him made her pulse race. He waved at her, but Zoe dropped her gaze to her lap. Since Zoe didn't want to encourage Romeo's advances, she told the taxi driver to step on it.

Chapter 3

On the outside, Casa Di Moda headquarters in the Milan city center was nothing special, but Zoe called the two-story property her second home. Housed in a brown brick building, with the name of the fashion house written on the windows in fine script, the decor was clean and simple.

Breezing through the front door, Zoe smiled and waved at her colleagues. The interior had bright colors, scrumptious chairs and couches, and vintage mirrors throughout the main floor. Oversize photographs of ad campaigns and fashion shows beautified the walls, and as Zoe entered the reception area, the tranquil atmosphere calmed her nerves. Despite the pain in her ankle, she moved with confidence.

The December program she'd created for Casa Di Moda was packed with creative holiday events, and Zoe was confident her boss would love it, especially the Men of Milan calendar. The idea had come to her days earlier after a loud, spirited conversation with her girlfriends on

FaceChat, and Zoe couldn't wait to pitch it at the morning staff meeting.

Reaching the conference room door, she smoothed her hands over her braids and the front of her dress. It had been one hell of a morning, but her day was about to get better. Excitement coursed through her veins. Cha-ching! Zoe had big plans for her bonus. After she paid her bills and bought her plane ticket to New York, she'd donate the rest of the money to her favorite charity. Last year, she'd organized a Christmas toy drive at the office, and it had been a success. This year, Zoe planned to do more.

For some strange reason, an image of Romeo Morretti popped into her mind, derailing her thoughts. She'd done nothing wrong, so why did she feel guilty about turning down his dinner invitation? Zoe had a bad feeling about him, just knew that he was as cocky as the tabloids said he was, so why did she regret not giving him her cell phone number? Had she made a mistake? During the taxicab ride, she'd read several articles about him on her tablet, and each story was more shocking than the one before. Born into one of the richest families in the country, Romeo had been educated in the finest schools and lived a life most people could only dream of. He owned real estate properties, premier restaurants, spas and fitness centers. Eight years after opening his company, Morretti Finance and Investments, his personal net worth had tripled. Not that Zoe was impressed by his staggering wealth. The most interesting thing she'd read about the brilliant businessman had nothing to do with his flamboyant lifestyle and celebrity friends. Every year, he donated millions of dollars to charity and even fed the homeless. *Maybe he's more than just a bad-boy bachelor*, she'd thought, staring at the images taken of him at local hospitals and orphanages. Maybe he has a heart.

Zoe shook her head to clear her mind. It didn't matter what she thought. She didn't have time to daydream about a man she'd never see again. She was late, and since every second counted, she gripped the door handle, turned it and peeked inside the conference room.

The blinds were drawn, allowing sunlight to fill the room, and decorative vases overflowing with peach and orange roses sweetened the air. Decorated in white with floor-to-ceiling windows, leather armchairs and contemporary art, the conference room was spacious and attractive. Fruit and pastry trays were on the table, and Zoe's mouth watered in anticipation.

Sighing in relief, Zoe eased open the door. Thankfully, Aurora had her back to the door and was furiously writing notes on the Smart Board. Her husband, Davide, was staring down at his iPad. With his clean-cut looks and salt-and-pepper hair, the executive vice president often joked about feeling old. But he had a youthful air, and everyone on staff loved him.

"Come here," Jiovanni mouthed. "I saved you a seat. Hurry up."

Hoping to go unnoticed, Zoe tiptoed across the room. The moment she sat down in the empty chair beside Jiovanni, Aurora called her name.

"Zoe, how nice of you to join us," she said, glancing over shoulder. "I hope my weekly staff meeting isn't interrupting your very busy schedule."

Her cheeks warmed and her stomach churned. Embarrassed that her boss was taking her to task in front of her colleagues, Zoe wore an apologetic smile. "Sorry I'm late Aurora, but I was in a—"

The designer spun around, startling her, and Zoe broke off speaking.

"Save it for someone who cares. We have work to do, and lots of it."

Feeling her mouth drop open, she stared at her boss with wide eyes. Aurora never raised her voice, let alone yelled at her, so Zoe was shocked by her tone. The designer wasn't just her boss, she was also a good friend, and her stinging retort hurt her feelings.

Aurora fussed with her multicolored scarf. Petite, with a brown pixie cut, olive skin and a slender frame, she had perfect posture and impeccable manners. "Zoe, I'm sorry I yelled at you." Sniffing, she dabbed her eyes with the back of her hand. "The last few weeks have been a nightmare..."

Her voice faltered, and she couldn't finish her thought.

Zoe straightened in her chair, tried to make sense of what was going on with her boss. Was Aurora having a mental breakdown? she wondered, scrutinizing the designer's appearance. Dark lines rimmed her eyes, but her black A-line dress complemented her shape, and the leopard-print heels she wore elongated her legs. Were the late nights, and early mornings, finally getting to her? Was she so overwhelmed with stress and fatigue she couldn't function?

Rising from his leather chair at the head of the table, Davide stood behind his wife and placed his hands on her shoulders. "Casa Di Moda is in trouble, and we need your help."

"What are you saying?" a graphic designer asked. "Is the company broke?"

Davide spoke in a solemn tone of voice. "No, but if we don't turn things around in the next three months, we'll have no choice but to file for bankruptcy."

The room was so quiet, Zoe could hear her heart beating inside her chest. Was this a joke? A trick? She wondered if the powerhouse couple were pulling her leg, and studied their faces for clues. They looked serious, sounded serious, too, but Casa Di Moda couldn't be in financial trouble. The line was popular; celebrities wore their designs to award shows, movie premieres and industry events. They'd recently landed a multiyear contract with an international film company to design costumes.

"That's impossible," Jiovanni argued, his short black curls flopping around his face. "We signed several deals this year, and high-end boutiques in Montreal, Dubai and Paris are chomping at the bit to carry our gowns as well."

Jiovanni had a fun-loving personality, an outrageous sense of humor and an infectious laugh. He loved fine wine, Italian rap music, and had a different woman on his arm every week. He liked to joke about marrying her one day, but he was the big brother Zoe never had, and she'd never ruin their friendship by getting involved romantically with him.

"The film company backed out of the deal weeks ago, but we didn't know how to tell you." Davide wore a sad smile. "You worked hard on the presentation, and we didn't want to disappoint you, especially after everything you've done over the years to help the line succeed."

"How could this happen? We've given our blood, sweat and tears to this company for years, and now we have nothing to show for it," grumbled the creative director.

"Casa Di Moda isn't the only company feeling the pinch," Aurora said. "People aren't splurging on designer labels like they used to, and according to official figures, clothing, shoes and jewelry fell another eighteen percent over the last nine months."

"Households are under increasing pressure as they wrestle with rising living costs," Davide added. "There's a lot of fear and uncertainty in the world right now. Consumers are being very conservative with their money, even the rich and famous."

Staff members grumbled and complained, bombarding Aurora and Davide with questions and concerns. Zoe couldn't speak. This couldn't be happening. Not to Aurora and Davide. They had big hearts, and she admired their tireless work ethic. Married for over a decade, the couple had no children, but referred to Casa Di Moda as their baby and treated everyone at the company like family. It was hard to listen to her colleagues bash them, but every time Zoe tried to come to the couple's defense, someone interrupted her.

"Everyone, please settle down. I'm still the boss, and I won't tolerate this kind of behavior at my company. If you can't be respectful, I'll have to ask you to leave."

Silence fell across the room as Aurora spoke, but tension and anger polluted the air.

"It will be business as usual around here during the holidays, but Davide and I will be away from the office a fair bit, so we'll need all of you to hold the fort while we're aggressively seeking new investors who'll help us take Casa Di Moda to the next level."

An associate designer raised her hand. "Are you planning to file for bankruptcy in the new year? Should we be looking for other jobs?"

Aurora stared down at the beige carpet, as if the answer to the question were written there. "I don't know," she said in a quiet tone of voice.

"Let's not dwell on the negative." Davide wore a broad smile. "Tonight's the premiere of *Amore in Tuscany*, and we expect to see all of you at Anteo spazioCinema. You can't get in the theater without your VIP pass, so guard it with your life."

For weeks, Zoe had been looking forward to the movie

premiere, but Aurora and Davide's announcement had soured her mood. Casa Di Moda collaborated with several European directors to design movie sets and costumes, and the success of the film could mean more business for the company. Since Zoe wanted to see the fashion house succeed, she'd post about the event again on her social media pages once she got to her office.

"One last thing," Aurora said, raising an index finger in the air. "If you have any ideas on how to help us turn things around and increase sales, please don't hesitate to share them with us. Speak up. We want to hear from you."

"I know a surefire way to boost sales and increase our popularity as well."

Everyone in the room cranked their heads in Zoe's direction but she wasn't at all intimidated. She had this. Knew what she was talking about. Had the numbers to support her argument. And she was excited to share her knowledge with her colleagues.

"You do?" Interest sparked in Davide's eyes.

"Well, don't keep us in the dark." Aurora spoke in a loud, animated voice. "What is it? What's your brilliant idea for saving Casa Di Moda?"

"Create a plus-size line for curvy women."

A scowl darkened Davide's face, and the smile slid off Aurora's thin pink lips.

"I don't design clothes for big girls," she spat. "And I never will."

"Why not?" Zoe pressed, curious why her boss had shot down her idea. "According to published reports, the average woman in the United Kingdom is a size fourteen, and I think it's high time we tap into that underserved and unappreciated market."

"We will not. I style women from size zero to size eight, and that's it."

"But women don't stop at size eight," Zoe argued. "We come in all shapes and sizes. As a woman with curves, I know firsthand how stressful it is to find attractive designer clothes in Milan. And from what I hear on social media, it's an issue all across Europe."

Aurora inspected her French manicure. "That's not my problem."

Zoe took a moment to collect her thoughts. Having had this conversation with Jiovanni numerous times before, she stared at her best friend for help, but he dodged her gaze. Undeterred, Zoe returned her attention to her boss, forgetting about everyone else in the room and speaking from the heart. "Aurora, you make the most beautiful clothes, and I'd kill to wear your designs but I can't because you don't make them in my size. Why not create clothes for everyone? Why not share your talent with the world?"

"Because if I do I'll never be taken seriously again as a designer. I'll be shunned by the entire fashion community. At this stage in my career that's a risk I can't afford to take."

"You're a designer, and no one can ever take that away from you."

"We could call the line, Chic and Curvy," proposed an intern with colored braces.

"I love it!" Zoe said, unable to hide her excitement. The expression on Aurora's face said *back off,* but she had to speak her mind. Wouldn't be able to live with herself if she kept her feelings bottled up inside. Buying clothes had been an issue ever since she'd moved to Milan. If not for Jiovanni making dresses for her to wear to industry events, she'd be stuck ordering clothes online from the States.

"You have a God-given talent," Zoe continued. "And it's time you share your gift with the world, namely curvy beauties like me. Hey, voluptuous women love fashion, too!"

Her joke fell flat, and for the second time in minutes, an awkward silence filled the air. Needing help, Zoe stared around the table at her colleagues, but everyone avoided her gaze. Undeterred, she flipped open her journal and reviewed her notes.

"I think the Men of Milan calendar promotion would tie in well with the launch of a plus-size line," she explained, continuing her pitch.

Aurora perked up. "A Men of Milan calendar? Sounds dreamy! Tell me more."

"Everyone who buys a Casa Di Moda gown during the Christmas holidays will receive a free calendar. People love getting free things, and I think this holiday promotion will be a hit."

"I love it," Aurora praised. "I think we should go all out. Let's hire male models to serve champagne and pose for pictures with customers as well."

Zoe tapped her pen on her notebook. "Christmas is several weeks away, but I'm going to get started on the Men of Milan today. We need to create buzz about our fabulous new holiday collection, and I think this is the best way to do it."

"Who do you have in mind for the calendar?" Davide asked, cocking an eyebrow. "Money is tight right now, so you'll have a very small budget for this project."

"No problem. Women love to see men in uniform, right, ladies?"

For the first time since the meeting started, her colleagues smiled and nodded.

"I'm going to hire some local models and dress them up as firefighters, paramedics, police officers and doctors.

I'm still working on the logistics, but I should have everything finished early next week."

"I want the proposal tomorrow," Aurora said.

Zoe gulped and her pen fell from her hands. *Twenty-four hours? Is Aurora out of her mind? That's not enough time to pull everything together!*

A cell phone rang, filling the air with a popular Italian pop song.

Smiling sheepishly, Davide took his cell out of his pocket, switched it off and put it on the table. "Great work, Zoe. I can tell everyone in here is really excited about this holiday promotion, and I'm pumped about it, too. Well done."

Thrilled that she had her bosses' support, Zoe jotted down ideas as they came to her. "How long will it take for the plus-size line to be ready?" she asked. "I think it would be cool if we had some women posing in Casa Di Moda gowns draped all over the models, don't you?"

Anger flashed in Aurora's eyes, and she spoke through clenched teeth. "We're not doing the plus-size line. Just the calendar. Got it?"

Worried she'd lose her temper if Aurora yelled at her again, Zoe picked up her glass and sipped her water. The self-made woman struck the fear of God in people, but Zoe wasn't going to let anyone disrespect her. "I'm disappointed that you won't consider my suggestion, but you're the boss, and I respect your decision," she said with a shrug. "If you don't want to expand the line and increase sales, there's nothing I can do."

Aurora seemed to shrink right before Zoe's eyes. With her head down and her shoulders hunched, she looked fragile and scared. Turning her face toward the windows, she gazed at the sky and fiddled with her wedding ring.

For all her wealth and success, she was stubborn and insecure, and Zoe had never pitied anyone more.

"As you all know, the Christmas Wonderland Ball will be held on December 20, and I don't have to tell you how important this event is for Casa Di Moda. Everyone who's anyone will be there, and it's a great networking opportunity for us all."

"How many tables will we have this year?" asked the human resources director, straightening in her chair. "Is everyone on staff invited?"

Aurora and Davide shared a troubled look, and Zoe knew the couple was about to share more bad news with the staff. Every year, famous names from fashion, film, politics, business and the world of sports attended the black-tie event, which raised millions of dollars for the local children's hospital in Milan. It had the most expensive and coveted tickets of the year, and Zoe was looking forward to attending her first Christmas Wonderland Ball.

"I wish everyone could go, but the cost of the ball has dramatically increased this year to 100,000 euros a table. Only the executive team can go," Aurora explained.

"That's all for today, everyone." Davide opened the door. "Back to work."

Staff members filed out of the room wearing long faces, and Zoe couldn't recall ever feeling so low. She wanted to stay behind to speak to Aurora privately, but decided against it. Now wasn't the right time. Filled with sympathy, Zoe watched the couple embrace. It was bad enough Casa Di Moda was struggling financially, and since she didn't want to make things worse for Aurora and Davide by arguing with them about expanding the line, Zoe grabbed her things and hurried through the open door.

Needing a moment to catch her breath, Zoe ducked inside the ladies' room and locked herself in a stall. *If I'm a valuable member of the team why won't Aurora and Davide take my ideas seriously? And why did Aurora roll her eyes when I pressed her for details about the plus-size line? Does she want to save Casa Di Moda from bankruptcy or not?*

Zoe used the bathroom, then washed her hands. Deep down, she feared things were going to get worse at Casa Di Moda in the coming weeks, and wondered what that would mean for her future. *Will I have a job after the holidays? Will I be forced to leave Milan for good?*

As Zoe studied her reflection in the mirror, her mind flashed back to her conversation with Romeo Morretti that morning. A thought came to mind. He was a businessman with deep pockets who owned an investment company. Someone with billionaire friends and clients. Maybe if she reached out to him he could help Casa Di Moda— Zoe shook her head, told herself it was a bad idea. No good could come out of calling Romeo Morretti. From what she'd read about him, he was an opportunist who preyed on vulnerable people. Since Zoe didn't like playing with fire, she pushed the thought from her mind. Yanking open the door, she marched down the hallway toward her office, determined to finish her paperwork before the six o'clock movie premiere.

Chapter 4

"I come bearing gifts," Jiovanni announced, poking his head inside the door of Zoe's office on Thursday afternoon. Wearing a broad grin, his eyes alight with mischief, he strolled inside the room clutching a wine bottle in one hand and a garment bag in the other. "After that staff meeting from hell this morning, I figured you could use a pick-me-up, so I brought you a snack."

Hard at work at her desk, Zoe glanced up from the field sales report she was reading and put down her yellow highlighter. "When did Chianti become an afternoon snack?"

"When Aurora announced that Casa Di Moda was floundering and had the nerve to ask *us* to save it." His smile disappeared, and a frown crimped his lips. "I almost fell off my chair when she said profits were down eighteen percent from last year. Of course they're down! What does she expect? She's controlling as hell and stifling everyone's creativity."

All afternoon, Zoe had been holed up in her office, blogging, tweeting and posting about the premiere of *Amore in Tuscany* at Anteo spazioCinema. The response to her online messages on the Casa Di Moda social media pages was so overwhelming, Zoe knew the event was going to be a success. Celebrities would be in attendance, on hand to mingle with fans and pose for pictures. Zoe was pleased her hard work was paying off. She'd been promoting the event for weeks, and was confident her industry friends would come through for her in a big way at the premiere. In a good mood, she didn't want to rehash what had happened at the staff meeting, but it was obvious Jiovanni needed to vent. She set aside her report and gave him her full attention, even though she had a million things to do before calling it quits for the day.

"I'm so angry, I could punch something." Jiovanni put the wine bottle on the mahogany end table and chucked the garment bag on one of the velvet chairs. "My opinions and ideas aren't valued here, and it's frustrating."

Zoe wore a sympathetic smile. "I hear you, J, and I know how you feel."

"This goes down on record as being one of the worst days of my life," Jiovanni confessed, plopping down on the edge of the desk, his shoulders hunched in defeat. "And it's Aurora and Davide's fault. If they respected their staff, instead of treating us like a bunch of dumb schmucks fresh out of fashion school, Casa Di Moda wouldn't be in this mess."

"Don't hold back," she joked, hoping to make her best friend laugh. "Tell me how you really feel."

Hanging his head, he rubbed at his eyes. "For the last nine years, I've given everything to Casa Di Moda, and now I have nothing to show for it."

Filled with compassion, Zoe rose to her feet and came

around her desk. "Don't say things like that." To comfort him, she rubbed his back. "All isn't lost. We'll help Aurora turn things around, and this time next year, Casa Di Moda will be more popular than ever."

"How? How can we make a difference when Aurora is stubborn, and closed-minded?" His voice was resigned, and his expression was grim. "I want answers, Zoe. Tell me how we fix things. How do we save this company and our careers?"

Stumped, Zoe didn't know what to say in response. Seconds passed, but nothing came to mind. Her thoughts returned to the staff meeting, and Zoe mentally reviewed everything that was said and done inside the conference room.

"I thought so. You don't know what to do, either."

"You're right, I don't, but I'm not giving up. I'm committed to Casa Di Moda, and I want to see it succeed."

Jiovanni spoke through clenched teeth. "And I don't?"

Silence descended on the room.

"What happened this morning?" Zoe asked, still bothered by his lack of support at the staff meeting. Educated and well-read, Jiovanni had an opinion about everything, so his silence during the discussion had bothered her. "Why did you leave me hanging? Why didn't you say anything when I lobbied for a plus-size line to be added to the holiday collection?"

"Because I knew Aurora would never go for it. You don't think I've tried to talk to her about expanding the woman's line a million times before? Well, I have, and the last time I submitted a detailed proposal, she tossed it in the trash." Jiovanni dusted his hands, as if they were covered in sand, and fervently shook his head. "Zoe, I don't know about you or anyone else on this sinking ship, but I'm done."

Zoe raised an eyebrow. "What are you saying?"

"That it's time I branched out and did my own thing in the fashion world."

"But you don't have enough money saved up yet to rent a space," she reminded him, recalling the conversation they had weeks earlier about his long-term goals.

"I know, but I'm sick of twiddling my thumbs. I'm just as talented as Aurora, and if I work my ass off, Designs by Jiovanni will be a household name in no time."

"I believe in you, J. You can do anything you put your mind to."

Seizing Zoe's hand, Jiovanni pulled her into his arms and held her close to his chest. He danced around the room, expertly dodging the furniture, then lifted her up in the air. "Jiovanni, stop!" she yelled, scared he'd lose his footing and drop her on the carpet. She'd taken two Asprin at lunch, and her ankle wasn't hurting her anymore, but she didn't want to do anything to aggravate it. "What are you doing? This isn't *Milan Dance Championship* and you're not a professional dancer, so put me down right *now.*"

"What do you mean, what am I doing?" he repeated, flashing a toothy smile. "I'm dancing with the most beautiful woman in Milan, and it's the best feeling in the world."

Zoe sighed in relief when her feet touched the ground. She swatted his shoulder. "Don't do that again. I almost had a heart attack when you picked me up, and I'm only thirty-two!"

"Quit playing. You know you loved it." Lowering his face to hers, he kissed her forehead. "I love holding you in my arms, Zoe. You know that."

His fingers grazed her forearm. He was too close for comfort, moving nearer to her, and Zoe feared he was going to do something crazy like kiss her. That would ruin everything. They were friends and nothing more.

She didn't want a romantic relationship with Jiovanni. Not today, not ever. Feeling trapped, she ducked under his arms and slid behind one of the chairs.

Her computer pinged, informing her that she had a new email message, and Zoe returned to her desk. These days Jiovanni was more flirtatious than ever, and she wondered if it had anything to do with his longtime girlfriend dumping him weeks earlier. To cheer him up she'd brought him home-cooked meals, wine and an armload of action movies.

"You and I make a great couple."

His gaze bore down on her, and a lascivious grin spread across his mouth.

"Everyone thinks so, even my nonna, and she's never liked any of my girlfriends."

To lighten the mood, Zoe cracked a joke.

"I'd never dream of arguing with your dear, sweet nonna," she said, making her eyes wide. "But the next time you want to re-create something you saw on your favorite dance show, find another partner, because I prefer having my feet on the ground, not suspended in midair."

Jiovanni stuck out his tongue and Zoe laughed. She could never stay mad at him; he made life fun, and she enjoyed his company so much they spent most of their free time together, much to his nonna's delight.

"You know what they say about male fashion designers, don't you?"

Zoe wore a blank expression on her face. "No. What?"

"They're the world's best lovers."

"According to who? You and the womanizers in your bad-boy posse?"

"My posse? Can't say I've ever heard that expression before," he said with a hearty laugh. "You kill me, you know that? I just love your sass and wit."

"Good, so you won't mind when I ask you to leave."

"So, that's how it is? I bring you wine, and you show your appreciation by kicking me out. That's cold. What's up with that? I thought you were my girl?"

"I am, but you have to go. You're distracting me, and I have tons of work to do." Zoe accessed her email account from her computer and read her newest message. "I have to finish planning the Men of Milan calendar, but we'll meet up later at the premiere. I'll save you a seat."

"No, don't. I have plans tonight, and they don't involve Casa Di Moda."

"You're not going to the movie? Why not? Aurora's expecting everyone to be there."

"She doesn't run my life, and there's no way in hell I'm canceling my date."

"But the after-party's at Milano Cocktail Bar, your favorite spot in the city."

"Like I said, I have other plans." Jiovanni took his cell phone out of his pocket and swiped his finger across the screen. "I met a woman last night at the Blue Note jazz bar, and I'm taking her to the new French restaurant in the Bicocca."

As Zoe listened to Jiovanni boast about his flavor of the week, her gaze fell across the web page on her computer, and she clicked it. An image of Romeo Morretti filled her screen. At lunch, as she'd sat at her desk eating the steak panini she'd ordered from a nearby deli, she'd read several articles about him, and even watched a documentary about his family. The Morretti family was an accomplished, successful bunch who donated their time, money and resources to worthy causes. But it seemed the more money Romeo made, the more ostentatious he was. Sure, he gave generously to charity organizations, but former employees painted him in a bad light.

And they weren't the only ones.

The interview his ex-fiancée had given to the tabloids was so outrageous, Zoe had abandoned her lunch and soaked up every juicy word. There were thousands of pictures of him online with his billionaire clients, supermodel dates and equally attractive family members. To her surprise, Romeo traveled more than a flight attendant. He was in Spain when his brother Emilio won his fifth Formula One championship, on hand when his cousin Demetri smashed another baseball record in the Windy City, at the opening of Dolce Vita Dubai to support his cousin Nicco, and the dutiful best man at his brother Markos's glamorous, over-the-top wedding in LA.

Zoe wet her lips with her tongue. Staring at the images of Romeo, she decided the photographs didn't do him justice. They failed to capture his energy, his zest for life. Truth be told, she was intrigued by him. He was such a force, so charismatic, she couldn't get him out of her mind. No surprise. Like every other woman in the city, she was attracted to his dashing good looks. Not that it mattered. Nothing would come of it. They didn't travel in the same social circles, and Zoe had a better chance of winning *Milan Idol* than making a love connection with one of the richest men in the country.

"Before I go, I want you to check out these outfits I designed specifically for you." Jiovanni grabbed the garment bag off the chair, unzipped it and marched around the desk. His confidence was evident in his broad I'm-the-man grin. "*Mi amore*, prepare to be blown away..."

Finding clothes that fit her hourglass figure in local stores was impossible, but Zoe could always count on Jiovanni to hook her up. Raised by a single mother and three older sisters, he understood women and appreciated the female body. From the moment Aurora had introduced them they'd clicked, and when his mother died unexpectedly last summer they'd grown even closer. He'd said she was his rock, the only person he trusted explicitly. His words had touched her heart. They'd never be lovers, but they'd be friends for life.

"What do you think? Did I hit it out of the park, or completely miss the mark?"

Zoe admired the outfits. Each one was impressive, and she couldn't decide which one she liked best—the beaded dress with the plunging neckline; the one-shoulder gown with the frilly red bow, or the navy pantsuit with the floral-print design along the waist. Overcome with emotion, Zoe gave him a hug and a kiss on the cheek. "Thanks, Jiovanni. I love all of them, and I'm honored to wear your amazing designs."

Dropping into a chair, he clasped his hands behind his head and crossed his legs at the ankles. "Prove it. Try them on, *mi amore*. Go ahead. Give me a show."

"With pleasure." Zoe grabbed the garment bag, draped it over her forearm and entered the bathroom. Much to Jiovanni's delight, she modeled each outfit, but when she sashayed out of the bathroom in the navy pantsuit, he cheered.

"That's it," he said, jumping to his feet. "*That's* what you should wear tonight."

"Are you sure it's not too sexy?" Zoe adjusted her cleavage.

"You have a great body and beautiful décolletage, so flaunt it." Jiovanni wore a proud smile. "I love to see you in my clothes. You make them come alive."

To complete her look, Zoe opened the closet and searched through her wooden jewelry box for the right accessories. Zoe often went straight from work to industry functions, and had everything she needed at her disposal.

Taking Jiovanni's advice, she selected teardrop earrings and a rhinestone necklace and bracelet. As she did her hair and makeup, he snapped pictures of her with his cell phone. With billions of people on social media every day, Zoe knew how important it was to give fans an intimate, behind-the-scenes look at Casa Di Moda and encouraged him to upload the images immediately.

"You look incredible," Jiovanni praised. "All eyes will be on you at the premiere."

Putting on her stilettos, Zoe admired her appearance in the full-length mirror beside the bookshelf. She felt so-phisticated in her chic ensemble, and Zoe was so anxious to hit the red carpet at Anteo spazioCinema, she decided to call it a day. The premiere didn't start for another three hours, but she wanted to get there early to live-stream interviews with the cast. As publicity director it was her job to promote Casa Di Moda, and she couldn't pass up the opportunity to rub shoulders with A-list celebrities, entertainment reporters and TV personalities.

Her desk phone buzzed, and the receptionist's voice filled the office.

"Hi, Zoe, sorry to bother you, but I need you at reception. You have a visitor."

Jiovanni rose to his feet. "Duty calls, huh?"

"Hopefully it's the blogger I spoke to yesterday," Zoe said, logging off her computer. "I want her to do a piece on Casa Di Moda and invited her to come by today for a tour."

Zoe grabbed her purse, turned off the lights and waved goodbye to Jiovanni. Hustling toward the reception area, she mentally rehearsed what she was going to say to the popular fashion blogger. Zoe hoped the online article would help boost sales, because just the thought of losing the best job she'd ever had made sadness fill her heart.

Chapter 5

The Casa Di Moda reception area was noisier than a train station, and the scent of coffee and expensive perfume wafted through the air. Telephones buzzed and staff members chatted in the hallway. Deliverymen shuffled in and out, carrying oversize boxes and packages.

As Zoe reached the entrance, she noticed a gift bag, a flower bouquet on top of the U-shaped desk and a mountain bike with a gigantic red bow propped against the far wall.

"Great, you're here," the receptionist said brightly, gesturing to the items with a nod of her head. "These things are for you. Do you want me to help you carry them to your office?"

"They are? But I didn't order anything online. Where did they come from?"

A slim man with a thick mustache appeared at Zoe's side and bowed in greeting. "Ms. Smith, these gifts are

from Mr. Romeo Morretti. His sincere hope is that everything is to your liking."

Stunned, all Zoe could do was nod in response. Peeking
inside the bag, she pushed aside the tissue paper. Her eyes
wide with disbelief, she admired each item—the crocodile
leather, Chanel handbag with the shiny diamond clasp,
the floral-print dress almost identical to the one she was
wearing that morning, and a Samsung cell phone and tablet. *Why would Romeo do this? I caused the accident, not
him, so why did he buy me thousands of dollars' worth of
gifts?* Her head was spinning as she struggled to understand what the gentleman was saying.

"Mr. Morretti wishes to extend his deepest apologies
for the incident that happened this morning, and hopes
that you will accept these presents as a sign of his deep
remorse."

"What incident?"

Aurora appeared at the reception desk with Davide at
her side. The couple wore designer outfits and sidled up
beside her, asking a million questions.

"What's this about?" Aurora asked, flinging her cash-
mere shawl over her slender shoulders. "What happened
between you and Romeo Morretti this morning?"

Zoe hadn't planned to tell anyone about her ill-fated
run-in with the business tycoon, not even her family.
Images of her parents, Reuben and Collette Smith, and
younger sister, Shelby, popped into her mind. Her mom and
dad were happily retired from their jobs, and her twenty-
six-year-old sister was a graduate student. During the staff
meeting, Aurora had made it clear there wasn't enough
money for a Christmas bonus. Without it, Zoe wouldn't
be able to go home for the holidays and didn't know how
she was going to break the news to her family.

As Aurora questioned her about Romeo Morretti, Zoe's

thoughts wandered. In September, she'd returned home to celebrate her parents' thirty-fifth wedding anniversary, but three days after arriving in Long Island she'd wanted to cut her one-month vacation short. Had actually considered returning to Milan to attend Fashion Week instead. Zoe couldn't go anywhere without her ex-boyfriend, Khalil Tisdale, nipping at her heels. Worse still, her mother adored him and his parents, and invited them over for dinner every evening. It didn't matter how many times she told Khalil that they were over, he wouldn't let her be. He was a successful orthodontist with a thriving medical practice. But he called her several times a day, showed up at her parents' house unannounced and wrote her love letters. They were over, and nothing he said or did would ever change that; still he pursued her relentlessly.

Fond memories filled her heart when she thought about her first love. Zoe was proud of Khalil and everything he'd accomplished, but she had no desire to rekindle their romance. All her life, she'd longed to travel abroad and experience different cultures and she'd refused to let anyone—not even her college sweetheart—stand in the way of her dreams.

"Earth to Zoe." Aurora waved her bejeweled hands in the air. "Tell us what's going on. We're dying to know about your run-in with Romeo Morretti."

Feeling trapped, she reluctantly told the couple about the accident, but left out the part about Romeo's dinner invitation. The less they knew about her interaction with the financier, the better. Aurora was obsessed with the rich and famous, and Zoe didn't want her boss to get the wrong idea about her and Romeo. "Thankfully, I wasn't hurt," she said with a sad smile. "My bike was totaled, but that was the worst of it."

Aurora gasped. "Good God, Zoe, how terrible! Why didn't you say anything?"

"It sounds worse than it was. I'm fine."

"Grazie a Dio!" she exclaimed. "I can't believe you were in a car accident this morning, but still came to work. You should have gone to the hospital to get checked out."

Zoe shook her head. "No way. I'm a New Yorker. I'm strong and resilient."

"Thank God you're okay. I don't know what we'd do if anything ever happened to you," Davide said in a solemn tone of voice. "You're an important part of the Casa Di Moda family. We don't want to lose you."

"I second that." Nodding, Aurora gave Zoe a one-arm hug. "You're the hardest-working employee we have, you've established a strong online presence for the company, and you've made the brand cool among millennials. We're fortunate to have you on board, Zoe."

Zoe was embarrassed by the couple's effusive praise and wished they'd stop showering her with compliments. The receptionist was listening in, and she was afraid the loquacious single mom would gossip to the rest of the staff about what Aurora and Davide had said. That would be a disaster. Jiovanni and the other associate designers were already upset, and Zoe didn't want them to feel worse.

"Now, back to you and Romeo Morretti." Aurora linked arms with Zoe and dropped her voice to a whisper. "What's he like? Does he smell good? What was he wearing this morning? Armani or Kenneth Cole?"

"I-I-I don't know," she stammered. "We only talked for a few minutes."

"Ms. Smith, Mr. Morretti wanted you to have this."

The gentleman reached into his jacket pocket, took out an envelope and offered it to Zoe, but Aurora plucked it out of her hand.

"I'll read it to you. You've had a stressful day, and I don't want anything to upset you."

Before Zoe could protest, Aurora ripped the envelope, took out the card and shrieked in a high-pitched voice in Italian about Zoe being rich.

I'm rich? What is she talking about? Zoe thought, bewildered by her boss's odd behavior.

Aurora was gesturing wildly with her hands, speaking so fast in Italian Zoe didn't understand a word she was saying. "What is it? Why are you screaming? What does the card say?"

Everyone in the reception area was watching them, and the gentleman's face was red.

"You struck pay dirt! Literally. Romeo Morretti just financed your future!"

What? Perplexed, she shook her head. Prying the envelope out of her boss's hands, Zoe realized the piece of paper she'd been waving around was a bank draft, and stared at the check. Zoe choked on her tongue. Rubbing her eyes, she counted the number of zeroes—twice—to make sure she hadn't made a mistake. A hundred thousand euros? What for?

"I have to return this. I can't keep it." Zoe glanced around, searching the reception area for Romeo Morretti's employee, but he was gone. Unsure of where Morretti Investments was, Zoe asked the receptionist to find the address online and waited patiently for her to locate it.

Drumming her fingernails on the desk, Zoe imagined what would happen when she saw Romeo again. Would she be calm and composed this time, or a tongue-tied fool? It was hard not to get flustered when he stared at her. His gaze was unnerving and intense, and his boyish smile could melt the ice around any woman's heart.

"Keep the gifts and the check. You earned it."

Earned it? It was an accident, not a setup! Again, Zoe was bewildered by Aurora's words. Surely she didn't mean it. Furthermore, what kind of person would Zoe be if she took the money? She wouldn't be able to live with herself if she did; guilt would eat her alive.

"Romeo Morretti struck you with his car, and you deserve to be adequately compensated," Aurora continued in a haughty tone of voice. "To be honest, a hundred thousand euros isn't enough money for your terrible pain and suffering."

Zoe frowned. *What pain and suffering? I'm fine!*

"I second that," Davide agreed. "Call Romeo Morretti and demand ten million euros."

"No way! That's crazy. I could never do that."

"If he refuses to pay, take him to court." Dollar signs flashed in Aurora's hazel eyes, and a smirk curled her lips. "You'll definitely win, and when you do, you can use your settlement money to invest in Casa Di Moda. It's a win-win for everyone!"

In businessman mode, Davide confided in Zoe about his meeting with bank officials yesterday, and the stress he was under to find new investors. Listening to him, Zoe was convinced that Aurora was making a mistake about the plus-size line. If they launched the line, and it did well, investors would come running. It wasn't the time or the place to broach the subject, but she decided to speak to her boss again tomorrow in private.

"Rosannah, can you do me a favor and put these things in my office before you leave?"

"No problem," the receptionist said with a curt nod. "I'll do it now."

"Thanks. I better get going or I'll be late for the premiere." Anxious to leave, Zoe took the piece of paper the receptionist gave to her and waved goodbye. "I'll see you guys later."

Aurora slid in front of her, blocking her path to the door, a defiant expression on her face. Looking chic in her backless ivory gown, she'd accessorized the dress with diamond jewelry, satin pumps and a chain-link purse. "Don't be silly. We'll drive you to Morretti Finance and Investments. It's the least we can do. You've had a very rough day."

"No, thank you. I don't want to inconvenience you. I'll just take a cab."

Davide took his car keys out of his pants pocket. "It's no trouble at all."

"We're taking you, and that's final." Aurora linked arms with Zoe. "I've always wanted to meet Romeo Morretti, and this is my big chance."

"You have?" Making her eyes wide, she faked a look of surprise. "Why?"

"Isn't it obvious? He's a smart, influential businessman with friends in high places, and we could use someone like him in our corner."

A cold chill stabbed Zoe's body. *Oh, no*, she thought, panic rising inside her chest.

They're going to ask Romeo for a loan, or worse, beg him to introduce them to his billionaire clients. Either way, Zoe was screwed, and as the couple hustled her out the front door, she couldn't help feeling like the sacrificial lamb.

Chapter 6

The offices of Morretti Finance and Investments was in a prestigious neighborhood in Milan on a tree-lined street teeming with fancy restaurants, supermarkets, art galleries and boutiques. Exiting Davide and Aurora's SUV, Zoe noticed there were beautiful cars, people and buildings everywhere. The sun was low, the traffic was light, and the sidewalks were overrun with millennials in search of the perfect place to eat, drink and party.

"Give my regards to Mr. Morretti!" Aurora shouted out the passenger-side window, cupping her hands around her mouth. "Convince him to invest in Casa Di Moda!"

Zoe nodded, but she had no intention of fulfilling her boss's request. In a stroke of good luck, the couple had forgotten their press passes for the movie premiere at the office, and since they had to return to the fashion house to get them, they couldn't accompany Zoe inside Morretti Finance and Investments. "Bye. Thanks for the ride. See you soon."

"Remember what I said." Aurora fervently nodded her head. "I'm counting on you."

Waving, Zoe escaped inside. On the drive over, Aurora had talked nonstop about her problems with the associate designers. As Zoe sat quietly in the backseat, she'd learned some valuable information about the fashion house. Information that made her body tense and her pulse race. Jiovanni was right. Casa Di Moda was on the brink of financial ruin, and if Aurora and Davide didn't change for the better, the fashion house wouldn't survive the next quarter.

Zoe entered the reception area and took in her elegant surroundings. Designer furniture, gleaming wood floors, sultry lighting and a granite bar filled the space. It looked more like a gentleman's club than an office, and the tantalizing aroma in the air made Zoe's mouth water. The office was quieter than the public library, and the receptionist was standing at attention at the glass desk, her bright smile showcasing every tooth.

Seeing photographs of Romeo with socialites and famous Italian actresses hanging on the ivory walls, Zoe wondered if everything she'd read about him online was true. Did he have a roving eye? Had he cheated on his ex-fiancée repeatedly? Was he deathly afraid of commitment?

Zoe cleared her mind. It didn't matter what Romeo did in his personal life; it was none of her business. Furthermore, she hadn't come to his office to have a heart-to-heart conversation with him about his past. She'd come to return the check, and once she did she was leaving.

Nervous anticipation coursed through Zoe's body as she approached the front desk. Deep down, she was excited to see Romeo again. Odd considering how they'd met, but the articles she'd read about him had piqued her interest. Of course she was curious about him. Everyone in the country was; she was no different. He was a gorgeous specimen of a man who was as successful as he was charming. Although Zoe had no intention of telling him about the problems at Casa Di Moda, she sensed he was exactly what the fashion house needed. An investor who was tough and tenacious, who wasn't afraid to take risks or shake things up. To please her boss, she'd get Romeo's card and pass it along. But that was it. She was the PR director at Casa Di Moda, not the CEO, and it wasn't her job to find investors.

"Hello. I'm Zoe Smith, and I'm here to see Mr. Morretti," she said in a confident voice.

The brunette consulted her leather-bound book. "Is he expecting you?"

"No, but I have something important to return to him, and it can't wait."

"I'm sorry, Miss, but Mr. Morretti is in a web conference and he can't be disturbed."

Zoe was disappointed, but she nodded her head in understanding. Opening her purse, she took out the envelope that had been delivered to her office and wrote a short note on the back. "Can you see to it that Mr. Morretti gets this letter—"

Hearing someone call her name, she broke off speaking and glanced over her shoulder. The pen fell from her hands. Zoe spotted Romeo standing in the corridor and swallowed a moan. *Holy hotness! Diavolo Sexy indeed!* For a moment she couldn't speak, could only stare at him. Romeo wore a suit like it was nobody's business. He looked more like an Armani model than a world-renowned financier. He had salon-ready hair, a cool, laid-back vibe and a killer bod. What more could a girl want?

Butterflies swarmed her stomach, but his smile instantly put her at ease. Zoe was determined to keep her wits about her, wasn't going to get flustered or tongue-tied in his presence like she had that morning at the taxi stand. His citrus cologne washed over, flooding her body with lust. Instead of crashing through the emergency exit and flagging down a taxi, Zoe walked toward him. Ignoring her sweaty palms and wobbly legs, she moved through the reception area with poise and grace.

"This is a pleasant surprise. Welcome to Morretti Investments, Zoe." Lowering his head, he took her hands in his and kissed her on each cheek. "You look sensational, even more beautiful than you did this morning. Where are you going all dressed up?"

"To a movie premiere, and I'm pressed for time, so I'll make this brief."

"Did you receive the gifts I had delivered to your office this afternoon?"

His enthusiasm was contagious, his tone endearing, and his sincerity touched her heart. Maybe she was wrong. Maybe he wasn't as bad as the tabloids made him out to be. If he was a jerk, like the gossip magazines claimed, he wouldn't have bought her presents—presents she didn't deserve. "Yes, and to be honest, I was stunned when I saw them."

"Do you like the bike?" he asked, touching her forearm. "It's the Mercedes-Benz of mountain bikes. The manager at the sporting goods store assured me you'd love it. Do you?"

"Yes, thanks. I'm sure I'll get plenty of use out of it." Zoe handed him the envelope. "I came here to thank you for the gifts and to return the check. I can't accept it."

His smile disappeared. "Please keep it. It's my way of making amends for this morning."

"You don't need to. I caused the accident, not you."

"The media aren't going to see it that way. They're going to blame me. Since I don't need any more bad press, I'd really appreciate if you cashed the check *and* kept quiet."

His words were a slap to the face, a powerful blow

she hadn't seen coming. The check was a bribe. Hush money. His way of buying her silence. "This is crazy," she said aloud. "Is that how you deal with your problems? By throwing money at them?"

"Yes, as a matter of fact it is." Sadness flashed in his eyes. "Unfortunately, I've learned over the years that most people are driven by the almighty dollar, so I decided to cut you a check and have it delivered to your office instead of waiting to hear from your attorney."

Shocked by his words, Zoe shot him an angry look. "I can't be bought."

"So, you're *not* selling your story to the highest bidder? Why not? Everyone else does."

"I'm not everyone else."

"Do us both a favor and cash the check. I'll sleep better if you do."

"I don't want your money," she snapped, feeling her temperature rise.

"Famous last words…"

"You don't believe me?" To prove it, Zoe tucked her purse under her arm, raised the envelope in the air, and ripped it in half. Wearing a cheeky smile, she dumped the pieces into his palm, then flipped her braids over her shoulders. Speaking in Italian, she said, "Bye, Romeo. Have a nice life!"

Eager to leave him in her dust, she spun around and marched toward the glass door.

Romeo captured Zoe's arm, stopping her in her tracks, and she glared at him.

"Maybe I misjudged you—"

"Damn right you did. I don't want your money."

His face softened. "I'm sorry. Do you forgive me?"

Romeo pretended to wipe an imaginary tear from his eye, and Zoe giggled.

"You have the best laugh. It's warm, loud and lively," he said, caressing her arm.

His cologne washed over her, and her temperature spiked. *What's the matter with me? Why am I acting like I've never been in the company of a man before? And why the hell am I making googly eyes at him? Damn, I'm worse than those female paramedics!*

"Where is the movie premiere?" Romeo asked.

"Anteo spazioCinema."

Glancing outside the window overlooking the sidewalk, he cocked an eyebrow. "Where's your date? Isn't he waiting for you outside?"

"I don't have a date."

A grin dimpled his cheek. "You do now."

"No thanks. I don't need one. My colleagues will be at the movie premiere, and they're flying solo, too. We'll keep each other company."

"I look forward to meeting them."

"No offense, Romeo, but you have a lot of relationship drama, and I don't want any of your girlfriends hunting me down for hanging out with you."

"Everything you read in the tabloids isn't true," he countered.

"True, but if you were *my* brother, I'd sit you down and set you straight about women."

"And if I were your man?"

"As if you could be so lucky!" Zoe quipped. "Keep dreaming, Morretti!"

Romeo chuckled long and hard, and the sound of his hearty laugh made her smile.

"You didn't answer my question," he pointed out, stepping forward, a mischievous expression on his face. "If I were lucky enough to be your man, what would you do with me?"

Lock you in my bedroom and throw away the key!

Noise filled the air, drawing Zoe's attention across the room, and she peered over his shoulder. Attractive women in designer dresses and impeccably groomed men strode through the reception area. Romeo greeted them as if they were family members, rather than his employees. "I should go," she said, noting the time on the contemporary clock hanging on the wall. "The premiere doesn't start for a couple more hours, but I want to get there early."

"Zoe, I'd be honored to be your date tonight."

The matter decided, Romeo asked the receptionist to retrieve his briefcase from his office, and as he waited for her to return he showed Zoe his favorite photographs in the reception area. He told her personal stories about his celebrity friends, his family members. Zoe could tell by the warmth in his voice that he was proud of his successful cousins and siblings.

"I brought your coat and cell phone as well, Mr. Morretti."

Taking the items from his receptionist, he nodded and smiled. *"Grazie."*

Needing some fresh air, Zoe ordered her legs to move and marched out the front door. The breeze carried a heady scent and cooled her overheated body. She searched the street for a taxi, but didn't see any on the road. She suddenly feared she wouldn't be able to shake Romeo.

"This is going to be fun. I haven't been to a movie in years."

"The premiere of *Amore in Tuscany* is by invitation only," Zoe blurted out.

"Don't worry. The director is a personal friend of mine. He'll be thrilled to see me."

"Are you always this confident?"

Romeo winked. "I have every reason to be. I know everyone in this town."

"But you don't have a VIP pass," she pointed out. "You'll be turned away."

"No way. It's not going to happen. I have friends in high places."

"Is that supposed to impress me?"

"No. I'm just stating a fact. Furthermore, you strike me as the kind of woman who cares more about a man's heart than who he knows. Is that a fair assessment?"

Distracted by his closeness, she couldn't think straight, and like a balloon in the sky, her thoughts wandered. To regain control, Zoe took a deep breath and clasped her hands in front of her. Good. Now she couldn't rip his suit from his body and have her way with him. It was an outrageous thought, one that caused her mouth to dry and her sex to tingle.

"Right this way, Zoe. My Lamborghini is parked around the corner."

Zoe didn't move. She'd never brought a date with her to a work function, and wondered what her colleagues would think if she showed up at the theater with the bad-boy businessman. Though she knew what her boss would do. Aurora would take one look at Romeo, in his tailored designer suit and diamond watch, and break out in song. Arriving to the premiere with Romeo would definitely put her on Aurora's good side, but Zoe had mixed feelings about taking him up on his offer. On one hand, she was excited about spending the rest of the night with him, but she was worried about attracting unwanted attention. The media would be out in full force tonight, and Zoe shuddered to think what bloggers would write about her. They made an unlikely pair, and she could almost see the headlines now: Italian Heartthrob Arrives at Movie Premiere with American! Romeo Morretti Romances Plus-Sized PR Director! Opposites Attract in Milan!

"Zoe, what's wrong?" he asked, a note of concern in his voice. "Why are you stalling?"

"Because I'd rather go to the premiere alone."

"Why? What do you have against financiers? We need love, too, you know!"

A giggle tickled her throat. "You're ridiculous, you know that?"

"Please don't deny me the joy of escorting you to the premiere. I promise to be on my best behavior, and I won't give you any trouble whatsoever." He clasped his hands together, as if in prayer, and spoke in Italian.

Please, beautiful? You won't regret it. His voice was full of warmth, and his expression was sincere. "Fine, you can come, but no monkey business. Understood?"

"You have my word. I'll be a perfect gentleman."

Romeo squeezed her forearm, and her mouth dried.

"We should go," Zoe said, wishing her sultry, throaty voice didn't betray her need. "The theater's across town, and I don't want to be late for the premiere."

"As you wish, bellissima. And don't worry. I'll have you there in no time."

It took supreme effort, but Zoe fell in step beside him, matching him stride for stride. Romeo was, without a doubt, the sexiest man she'd ever met. And when he wet his lips with his tongue, Zoe moaned inwardly. Her palms were slick with sweat, and she was so nervous about being alone with him in his sports car, she was quivering. She'd been on numerous blind dates since moving to Milan, but none of the men she'd met excited her. They were all successful, clean-cut guys who were exactly her type. But there'd been no chemistry. No magic. No fireworks. No sparks. When Romeo placed a hand on her lower back, electricity shot through her veins. Zoe then knew she was in trouble.

Chapter 7

Romeo stood with Zoe and her colleagues at the wrap-around bar inside Milano Cocktail Bar listening to Aurora and Davide Bordellio entertain the group with titillating stories about last year's Christmas Wonderland Ball. He quickly decided he liked the couple. They finished each other's sentences, and were down-to-earth. The couple were friendly and sociable, and when they welcomed him to the "Casa Di Moda family," Romeo chuckled. "I had to practically beg Zoe to let me tag along, but I'm glad she eventually relented," he said with a grin. "Everyone's real laid-back, and I'm having fun."

Nodding, Zoe gestured around the room with her hands. "Everyone is. The dance floor's packed, guests are chatting and snapping selfies, and the line at the dessert table is out the door."

Romeo raised his glass to his mouth and tasted its contents, but his gaze never left Zoe's face. In her navy jumpsuit and studded pumps, her look was the perfect blend of sophisticated and sexy. Her outfit flattered her fine womanly shape, and her red-painted lips were a turn-on. Romeo noticed heads turn as Zoe swayed to the beat of the music playing in the lounge, and he stepped forward. He wanted to be as close to her as possible, and wanted everyone else in the lounge to know she was taken. Thoughts of kissing her ruled his mind, but Romeo didn't act on his impulses. He didn't want to blow his chance with her. If he came on too strong, she'd show him the door.

"This is one of the best lounges I've ever been to," Zoe said, swiveling her hips like a dancer in Rihanna's latest video. "DJ Bella is amazing. I love this set!"

Romeo swallowed hard. It was hard to focus, impossible not to stare when Zoe was moving her body in such an erotic way. She danced with such confidence that he couldn't take his eyes off of her or concentrate on what she was saying.

"I heard DJ Bella will be at the Christmas Wonderland Ball along with Andrea Bocelli and Il Divo," said one of Zoe's male colleagues. "It's going to be the party of the year."

Zoe's face lit up. "I'd do anything to see Il Divo perform live. I'm their biggest fan!"

Romeo finished his appetizers, then handed the empty plate to a server. A cut above the rest, Milano Cocktail Bar was the most popular restaurant-lounge in the city, and the Hollywood-theme decor was a hit among the crowd. There was a red carpet, shiny helium balloons, life-size cutouts of the characters in *Amore in Tuscany*, and film tape hanging from the ceiling. Romeo thought the movie was a predictable romance with a weak plot, but Zoe loved it. She had gushed about her favorite parts of the film as they'd driven from the theater to the lounge. The entire restaurant had been rented out for the after-party, and the space was packed with celebrities, business executives and entertainment reporters.

Aurora touched Romeo's forearm. "You should come to Casa Di Moda for a private tour. Davide and I are incredibly proud of our business and everything we've accomplished over the last nine years. We'd be honored to have you visit the fashion house."

Romeo considered her words. Mentally reviewing his schedule, he realized he had several meetings and a business lunch on Monday, but decided to juggle his schedule to accommodate Aurora's request. Not because he wanted a behind-the-scenes look at the fashion house, but because he wanted to see Zoe again. "I'm free on Monday at ten o'clock," Romeo said, consulting the calendar on his cell phone. "Would that work for you?"

Aurora bobbed her head. "I'll make it work."

"Great. After the tour we'll have lunch at the Four Seasons. My treat."

Everyone at the bar cheered except Zoe, and Romeo frowned. Bothered by her lackluster response, he studied the expression on her face. Why wasn't she excited? The Four Seasons restaurant, La Veranda, was a magnet for professionals, and Romeo was confident Zoe and her colleagues would love the eclectic menu and quiet ambience. "I hope you're the one giving me the tour," he whispered in her ear. "Because you're my favorite of the Casa Di Moda staff."

"I have meetings all morning, so I won't be back at the office until late."

Romeo kept his feelings in check. Played it cool. Pretended not to care even though he was disappointed. His emotions must have showed on his face, though, because Zoe smiled sympathetically and patted his forearm.

"Don't worry. You'll have a great time at Casa Di Moda. Aurora and Davide are awesome. They can answer any questions you have about the business."

Romeo nodded, but he wasn't going to Casa Di Moda on Monday if Zoe wasn't there. Bent on seeing her, he made up his mind to visit the fashion house in the afternoon, making a mental note to adjust his schedule. Listening to Zoe and her colleagues talk about their plans for the rest of the weekend, Romeo realized it was going to be hard to get close to her. To romance her. She had a busy social life, and everyone wanted to spend time with her. He was anxious to get Zoe away from her colleagues—especially the male associate designer who was staring at her cleavage—but before he could ask her to dance, she spoke to her friend.

"Let's check out the dessert table," Zoe proposed, linking arms with a graphic designer with frizzy hair and red eyeglasses. "I'm craving something sweet."

Look no further, Romeo thought, hiding a grin. *I can satisfy your sweet tooth and more.*

Applause and whistles filled the lounge, and Romeo glanced over his shoulder to see what the commotion was. He didn't recognize the scantily dressed women posing for pictures on the mezzanine, but Zoe did, and cheered as the trio sashayed into the lounge.

"The cast of *Guilty Pleasurers* just walked in, and they're wearing the outfits I sent them from Casa Di Moda's holiday line," Zoe explained.

Romeo had never heard of the show, but he wanted to know more about her, so he listened closely to everything she said about the program. It sounded silly, like one of the ridiculous shows his sister, Francesca, enjoyed watching, but he kept his thoughts to himself. Romeo was a news junkie, and wouldn't be caught dead watching reality TV.

But learning more about Zoe's interests and hobbies was the first step to achieving his goal, so he didn't judge.

"I'm going to snap some pictures of the cast, ask them to record a personal message for Casa Di Moda fans, then upload the images on our social media pages. Wish me luck!"

You don't need luck, Romeo thought, his gaze trailing her through the room. *You're likable and gregarious.* He watched Zoe and several of her female colleagues saunter through the lounge, chatting and laughing with guests, and hoped she'd be back soon. Romeo wanted to dance with her, liked the idea of being alone with her, holding her in his arms, even if it was only for a couple minutes— "Zoe likes assertive, take-charge guys, so quit playing it safe."

The sound of Aurora's voice broke into his thoughts. Cranking his head to the right, he noticed the fashion designer staring at him and pretended he didn't know what she was talking about. "Excuse me?"

"Don't play coy. You want her. Just admit it."

"Is it that obvious?" he asked with a sheepish smile.

"Yes, but don't feel bad. Zoe's a magnet who attracts male attention wherever she goes."

"You're her boss and mentor, but it sounds like you're also good friends."

"We are. I was one of the first people Zoe met when she arrived in Milan, and we instantly hit it off," she said, speaking with a broad smile on her face. "Despite our age difference, we have a lot in common and I value Zoe's opinion. She's wise beyond her years."

Romeo soaked up every word that came out of the fashion designer's mouth, committed every piece of information she shared to memory. "Does she have a boyfriend?" he asked, watching Zoe move around the lounge. She gave out hugs and kisses as if they were going out of style, but he enjoyed seeing her in action. Zoe was a force, so engag-

ing and appealing she turned heads all around the room.
"Is she dating anyone special right now?"

"No, but she has plenty of male admirers."

"Figures. Beautiful women always do."

"Zoe's more than just a pretty face, though…"

Tell me something I don't know— Romeo gripped his
glass so hard the veins in his hands throbbed. What the
hell? There were lots of celebrities in the restaurant, but
Romeo was shocked to see the goalkeeper for his favorite
football team talking to Zoe. Or rather, flirting with her.
The footballer was whispering in her ear, as if they were a
couple sharing a private joke. Loved worldwide, the athlete
had championship medals and more fans than Beckham.
*What does he want with Zoe? Is that the kind of guy she
likes? Athletes with tattoos and piercings?*

"She's talented and smart. We'll miss her dearly if she
leaves."

His ears perked up. "She's leaving? When? Why? Where
is she going?"

Glancing around, Aurora shielded her mouth with her
hand and spoke in a quiet tone of voice. "Zoe's here on a
work visa, and if I can't find new investors by the end of
the year, I'll have to close Casa Di Moda for good. She'll
have to leave Milan immediately."

"How many investors do you need?"

"As many as I can get, but…"

Romeo didn't hear a word Aurora said. His eyes tracked
Zoe around the room. He saw the goalkeeper take the bub-
bly PR director in his arms and dance cheek to cheek with
her. She was smiling and laughing. Romeo didn't like it
one bit. Wanted to break up their cozy slow dance. His eyes
narrowed. The footballer was stroking her shoulders and
hips, but Romeo forced himself to stay put. Not to react. He
wasn't the jealous type and never chased women down, but

Zoe made him act out of character. He wanted to protect her, to take care of her, and hated seeing her with another man. They'd known each other for less than twenty-four hours, so why was he acting like a jealous ex? Why did he want to rip her out of the goalkeeper's arms and hustle her back into his sports car?

"Romeo, if you ever need advice about how to woo Zoe, just give me a ring."

Aurora reached into her purse, took out a business card and stuffed it into his pocket.

"Call anytime. I'm just a phone call away."

"Thank you, Aurora. That's very kind of you."

Davide joined the conversation, echoing his wife's sentiments, and Romeo nodded politely. They needed investors and wanted to talk shop. But getting Zoe away from the touchy-feely goalkeeper was his focus, not saving a fashion house from financial ruin. Though he did like the idea of doing something nice for Zoe since she wouldn't accept his check, and considered investing on her behalf.

Wearing a wry smile, Romeo shook his head. He still couldn't believe she'd ripped up his check and thrown it in his face. He was used to women asking him for money and expensive gifts, not returning them. He respected Zoe for being a person of integrity and character. Not to mention fine as hell. She was a stunner, and like Cristal and Cuban cigars, impossible to resist.

Romeo felt his eyes bulge out of his head and a cold chill stab his flesh. *When it rains, it pours*, he thought, shaking his head. *Damn. What is Lizabeth doing here? Who invited her?* Had she discovered his whereabouts by perusing his social media pages? The more Romeo thought about it, the more he was convinced that Lizabeth had come to the after-party to make trouble.

Hours earlier, he'd asked Zoe to take a picture with him, and she'd declined.

"You don't strike me as the selfie type," she'd said, a what-are-you-up-to expression on her face. "So why do you want to take one with me?"

"Because I want to commemorate our first date." Grinning, he'd draped an arm around her waist and held her close to his side. "One day you're going to thank me."

Using his cell, he'd snapped the photograph and uploaded it to his FaceChat account, with the caption, "Zoe Smith, the Gold Standard of Beauty." Within minutes, hundreds of people had commented on his post, including several of Lizabeth's friends. Is that why she was at the party? To find out who Zoe was? He wouldn't put it past her. When they were dating, she used to snoop through his things and would cause a scene whenever he spoke to someone of the opposite sex. Lizabeth had been the one to call off their engagement, but she was bent on making his life miserable. He feared her sole purpose in coming to the party was to embarrass him.

Lizabeth waved, but Romeo ignored her. Her sheer dress had a plunging neckline and high slits and left nothing to the imagination. It was a wardrobe malfunction waiting to happen, and Romeo didn't want to be around when disaster struck. Because of Lizabeth's obsession with being famous, he was endless fodder for gossip columns, and Romeo was sick of it. In the modeling world, Lizabeth had quite the reputation, and he regretted ever helping her launch her career.

Romeo exited the lounge and strode through the restaurant. Out of the corner of his eye, he saw Zoe dancing with her colleagues and sighed in relief. The goalkeeper was at the bar, flirting with the female bartenders, and Romeo hoped the star athlete stayed there—and far away from

Zoe—for the rest of the night. Impressed by her knowledge of Italian history, world events and pop culture, Romeo wanted to know more about her. He hoped he could convince her to join him for a drink at his favorite bar when the after-party ended.

Also hoping to avoid his ex, Romeo entered the men's room and used the facilities. He washed his hands and stared at his reflection in the mirror. Faint circles lined his eyes, but he looked handsome in his Armani suit and navy tie, like a man who had everything. But it was a facade. The only people he could truly trust were his family, and he had very few real friends.

Exiting the bathroom, Romeo checked his cell phone for missed calls, and noticed he had a new text message from his brother. With three university degrees, and an implausibly high IQ, it was no surprise to anyone in the Morretti family that Enrique's media company, Icon Productions, had made the Forbes list for the fifth consecutive year.

Romeo read the message, and a frown wrinkled his brow. Enrique wanted to meet up tonight for drinks at Hollywood nightclub. He decided he would speak to Zoe before he responded to his brother's message. Happily engaged to his live-in fiancée, Enrique spent all of his free time with the talented art director. Romeo was lucky if he saw him once a month.

"What did you think of my interview in *Celebrity Patella* yesterday?"

Romeo kept his eyes on his cell phone, didn't bother to look at his ex and her minions. "I don't have the time to read tabloids. I have clients to meet, deals to close and millions to make."

"Whatever. Just have my money by Monday or the deal's off."

Confused, he glanced up from his cell. "There is no deal."

"Of course there is. Giuseppe called this morning and made me one hell of an offer." A smirk curled her lips. "He said if I scrap my tell-all book and sign a confidentiality agreement, you'll give me five million dollars *cash*."

Romeo cursed under his breath. He was angry that his publicist had struck a deal with Lizabeth behind his back, but wore a blank expression on his face. Didn't react when she gloated about the seven-figure deal. Romeo didn't want to hear any more. He'd heard enough. He wanted to return to the bar to hang out with Zoe, not argue with his ex-fiancée about money, but he couldn't resist setting her straight. "I'm not giving you another dime. Not today. Not ever."

Her face fell, and she stumbled over her words. "B-B-But, Giuseppe promised me—"

"I don't give a damn what Giuseppe said. There is no deal. And the next time you lie about me or my family, I'll sue you and your modeling agency."

Lizabeth bit her bottom lip. "You wouldn't."

"Think I'm bluffing? Try me."

Romeo returned her stare. Lizabeth was trying to take advantage of him, trying to bully him into giving her millions of dollars, but he wasn't going to let her win. After they broke up, she'd threatened to sue him, arguing she deserved to be financially compensated for the years they'd lived together at his palatial villa in Tuscany. Thankfully the judge had tossed out her case. At his sister's urging, he'd agreed to let Lizabeth keep the sports cars he'd bought her, and the ten-carat diamond ring he'd proposed with on her birthday.

"How can you treat me like this after everything we've been through? After everything I've done for you?" Lizabeth asked, shouting her words.

"You did me a favor calling off our engagement. I only wish you'd done it sooner..."

Romeo's gaze landed on Zoe, and he broke off speaking. Spotting the PR director moving through the lounge, he lost his train of thought. Couldn't focus on anything but the scintillating beauty.

"I called off our engagement because you cared more about your family and your stupid company than you did about me," Lizabeth complained. "What did you expect me to do? Sit around and wait for you to finally come to your senses?"

Romeo tuned her out, instead focusing his attention on Zoe. Tired of arguing with his ex, he marched through the lobby, determined to reach her before someone else whisked her away. "Zoe, where are you going?"

Her smile was so radiant and bright, his anger abated and a grin curved his mouth.

Taking her hand in his own, he gave it a light squeeze. "You're not going anywhere, Ms. Smith. You still owe me a dance."

"It's late, Romeo, and I'm beat. Maybe next time, okay?"

He didn't want her to leave and tried to persuade her to stay. "I'll drive you home."

Zoe yawned. "No, thanks. Lorenz lives near me, and we want to discuss work on the drive home."

She released his hand, and disappointment coursed through his body.

"I have to go," she said, raising her cell phone in the air. "Lorenz just texted me. He's waiting out front—he's anxious to leave."

Out of his peripheral vision, he saw Lizabeth headed his way and narrowed his eyes. There was no way in hell he was letting his ex anywhere near Zoe, and shielded the PR director with his body. Lizabeth was toxic, and he couldn't stand to be around her.

"Gold standard of beauty my ass." Cocking her head to the right, she glared at Zoe like a schoolyard bully looking for trouble. "You're pretty, but you're no Tyra Banks."

"Good, because I'm Zoe Smith. I wouldn't want to be anyone but me. I'm fabulous."

Romeo smiled. Not because Zoe had put Lizabeth in her place, but because of how damn good she looked doing it. Her head was high, her shoulders were pinned back, and she reeked of confidence. Zoe was in control, had the upper hand, and Romeo was impressed with how she carried herself. He stared at her with open admiration.

"Lizabeth, I'm the PR director for Casa Di Moda and I'm always on the lookout for captivating personalities to work with us." Zoe opened her purse, took out a glossy pink card and handed it to Lizabeth. "Call me."

A grin crept across Lizabeth's mouth as she read the information on the business card.

"I'd love to hire you for one of our upcoming fashion shows," Zoe said with a bright smile. "So give me a ring."

"We can talk now. Let's have a cocktail."

"I wish I could, but my ride is waiting for me outside."

Lizabeth tossed her silky brown locks over her shoulders. "Then I'll walk you to your car. You can tell me more about Casa Di Moda, because I'm *totally* intrigued."

"Sounds good." Zoe smiled and waved. "Bye, Romeo! Enjoy the rest of your night."

Panic ballooned inside his chest. He had to do something. Had to stop Zoe from leaving with Lizabeth. He didn't want his ex to poison Zoe's mind toward him, and feared what would happen if the two women were alone.

Romeo stepped forward, but Lizabeth slid in front of him, blocking his view of Zoe. Dumbfounded, he watched

Zoe leave the restaurant lounge with his ex-fiancée. Chatting a mile a minute, the women breezed through the door, oblivious to the wide-eyed expression on his face.

Raking a hand through his hair, Romeo cursed under his breath in Italian. He'd blown it with Zoe again. How was that possible? He was a Morretti. He never struck out with women, never failed to achieve his goal, regardless of what it was. But it had happened twice in one day.

Romeo fixed his tie and leveled a hand over his jacket. He had to redeem himself. Had to prove to Zoe that he was a good man. His confidence returned, and a grin crept across his lips. He'd seduce her, no doubt about it. Even if it meant pouring on the charm.

Chapter 8

The soccer ball sailed in the air at Parco Sempione and dropped onto the freshly cut grass, just inches away from where Romeo was standing. Moving quickly, he sprang into action. Dodging approaching defenders, he ran toward the net, bent on scoring another goal for his team. Filled with adrenaline, sweat coursing down his face, he carefully dribbled the soccer ball. Winded, Romeo scanned the field for Enrique, but he couldn't find his brother anywhere.

His heart was beating out of control, roaring in his eardrums, but Romeo ran harder, faster. At his yearly physical last month, his doctors had warned him about overexerting himself, encouraging him to take up golf, but football was his first love, and that would never change.

Using fancy footwork, he raced up the field, twisting and turning to avoid the burly midfielder with the death stare. Romeo kicked the ball with supreme force. Holding his breath, he watched it fly through the goalie's hands, hit the back of the net and fall to the ground.

Filled with pride, Romeo threw his hands in the air. Cheers erupted around him as his teammates celebrated his second goal of the game. Once a month, regardless of the temperature, Romeo and his friends played football at Parco Sempione. It was Milan's version of Central Park, and there was so much to see and do he often spent the entire day there. Nature lovers were cycling, jogging, playing Frisbee and flying handmade kites. It was noisy and crowded, and children were running in every direction. Romeo couldn't have asked for a better day.

"What a goal!" Enrique shouted, jumping onto his back. "You were amazing, bro!"

"Thanks, man. I learned from the best."

Grinning, he plucked at the front of his blue Manchester United jersey. "You're right. I *did* teach you everything I know about the game."

"I was talking about Immanuel."

A scowl curled his lips. "I should have known. You always liked him better."

"That's not true, but Sharpshooter looked out for me a lot when we were kids. I'm very grateful," Romeo explained. His brother, Immanuel, was a security specialist, who provided protection to high-powered people. "I was a wimp. If not for Immanuel, bullies would have kicked my ass up and down the school yard every day."

"And look at you now. You're one of the most successful businessmen in the country, a bona fide ladies' man and a hell of a football player, too." Enrique ruffled Romeo's dark brown hair. "Let's go grab a cold one. You've earned it."

Jogging across the field toward the picnic tables their teammates were eating at, Romeo heard laughter and the

distant sound of a guitar. He saw couples kissing and cud-
dling under maple trees and college students playing coed
rugby. A female with curly hair waved at him, but Romeo
dodged her gaze. She was attractive, sure, but she had
nothing on Zoe. The PR director was a knockout, desirable
in every way. He needed to see her again. It had been five
days since he'd gone for a private tour of Casa Di Moda,
and although they texted each other every day, it wasn't
enough. Did Lizabeth fill her mind with lies? Is that why
Zoe was keeping him at arm's length?

His week had been a disaster. He'd had a heated argument with Giuseppe for making an unauthorized deal with
Lizabeth behind his back; the local newspaper had done a
write-up about his car accident; and yesterday he'd arrived
at the office to find reporters camped outside Morretti Finance and Investments. They shouted his name, snapped
pictures of him every time he left the building and filmed
his every move. It was annoying, frustrating as hell for
his staff and clients, but there was nothing Romeo could
do about it. What had frustrated him more than anything
was that he'd made zero progress with Zoe since the after-
party at Milano Cocktail Bar.

What am I doing wrong? he thought, wiping his damp
face with the sleeve of his football jersey. *What do I have
to do to get through to Zoe? To make her see that I'm an
upstanding guy?* He couldn't shake the feeling that Lizabeth had screwed him over. She took pleasure in hurting
him, seemed to get off on making him suffer. He'd known
from the very beginning that the Norwegian model was
spoiled and high-strung. After years of her diva-like behavior, he'd had enough. Initially, he'd been shocked when
she'd called off their engagement, but deep down he'd been
relieved. Dating Lizabeth had been mentally, physically

and emotionally draining. Romeo would rather be celibate for the rest of his life than take his ex back.

For the second time in minutes, an image of Zoe filled his mind, and his thoughts returned to yesterday. He'd called Casa Di Moda to ask her out and ended up talking to Aurora instead. He'd been bummed to find out Zoe was in Florence for a photo shoot, but he enjoyed shooting the breeze with her boss. Eager to help, the fashion designer promised to talk to Zoe on his behalf and encouraged him to visit Casa Di Moda whenever he was in the neighborhood.

Romeo had to see Zoe. She was all he could think about, and he wanted to spend time with her. To stay connected to her, he followed her on social media, and seeing the pictures she'd posted that morning made Romeo desire her more than ever.

"I'm glad you talked me into coming down here today," Enrique said, opening the cooler. "I've had a hell of a week, and playing football with the guys is the ultimate stress reliever."

Starving after their marathon game, Romeo headed straight for the barbecue pit. The savory aroma in the air caused his stomach to grumble. Grabbing a metal serving spoon and a paper plate, Romeo filled it with the mouthwatering foods his friends had grilled for lunch.

Romeo sat down at a picnic table to eat. Everything was hot, seasoned to perfection, and he savored each and every bite. Pressed for time, he hadn't had anything for breakfast that morning, so he thoroughly enjoyed his first meal of the day. His friends cracked jokes and teased each other, and their hearty laughter created a lighthearted mood in the picnic area.

Enrique took the seat across from him. He was clutching his cell phone, and Romeo noticed his brother's eyes darken and wondered if he was having business trouble again. A rival entertainment company had lured away his best employee weeks earlier, and Enrique was still picking up the pieces of the executive's sudden departure.

"What's wrong? You look like you're about to blow a gasket."

"It's Isabelle…" Trailing off, he rubbed a hand along the back of his neck. "Lately, she's been pulling away from me, and I don't know why."

"Have you tried talking to her?"

"Yeah, but we end up fighting about it, then she storms out," he explained. "Last night, we got into it again, and Isabelle went to her parents' place to cool off. I've texted her several times to find out when she'll be home, but she hasn't responded."

"Man, quit sweating her. She'll come around, and if she doesn't you can always find someone else. I like Isabelle, but she's not the only beautiful woman in the world."

"I don't want anyone else. I want Isabelle. She's it for me, bro."

"Such devotion," Romeo drawled. "You need to ease up. You're trying too hard. You don't want her to think you can't live without her—"

"I can't. Isabelle is the best thing that's ever happened to me. I won't lose her."

"Damn, bro, you're gushing like a water fountain," Romeo teased, wiping his fingers with a napkin. "You're worse than Markos and Tatiyana, and they're newlyweds!"

"You don't understand, because you haven't met Mrs. Right yet, but when you do, you'll move heaven and earth to make her happy." Shrugging his shoulder, Enrique wore a sheepish smile. "I used to think Emilio and Immanuel were suckers for settling down and getting married. Now I can't wait to make Isabelle my bride. What can I say? The love bug bit me in the ass, and there isn't a damn thing I can do about it!"

Chuckling, Enrique put his cell down on the wooden table and picked up his fork.

"Are you still going to the Christmas and Cocktails event at the Armani Hotel Milano or have you changed your mind?" Romeo asked, reaching for his water bottle.

"I don't know. I was supposed to go with Isabelle…"

"Don't sweat it, bro. I'll go with you. I love networking with smart, talented people."

"With curves, right?"

"Absolutely. The curvier the better."

Laughing, the brothers bumped bottles, then guzzled down their drinks.

"How are you feeling? Any chest pains, muscle spasms or dizzy spells as of late?"

"No. I'm the picture of health. Doctor said so himself at my physical last month."

Romeo stared at the field, but he wasn't watching the coed rugby game. He was thinking about Zoe. What else was new? It wasn't every day he met a woman who piqued his interest. Just the thought of the vivacious PR director made an erection rise inside his Nike shorts.

His cell phone rang, and he glanced down at the screen. Raising an eyebrow, he cocked his head to the right, surprised to see Aurora Bordellio's name pop up on his phone. Why was the fashion designer calling him? Hope surged inside his heart. Was she with Zoe? Curious, he pressed the accept button and put his cell to his ear. "Hello, Mrs. Bordellio. How are you?"

"Romeo, why are you being so formal? Please, call me Aurora."

"Sure," he said, anxious to find out what she wanted. "What can I do for you?"

"My husband and I are hosting a dinner party tonight, and we'd love if you could join us. I apologize for the short notice. We've been insanely busy the last few days."

"Thank you for the invitation, but I have plans with my brother tonight—"

"Bring him with you!" Aurora offered, interrupting him. "Zoe's really looking forward to seeing you tonight. Don't tell her I told you this, but she has a *huge* crush on you."

His jaw dropped, but he asked the question circling his mind. "She does?"

"Yes, of course. Isn't it obvious? Zoe couldn't take her eyes off of you at the after-party."

Really? Romeo thought, scratching his head. *Then why is she playing hard to get?*

"Zoe's the perfect woman for you," she continued in a haughty tone of voice, as if she had the answers to all of life's mysteries. "She's sincere and loyal, and one of the most selfless women I know. Not to mention she's a total bombshell."

Romeo stared down at his cell. Aurora was laying it on thick, trying to convince him to pursue Zoe, even though he was already interested in her—luckily, he was amused, not annoyed. He liked Aurora and Davide, and appreciated her unexpected dinner invitation. "What time is dinner?"

Aurora hollered like a game show contestant who'd won the grand prize. "Seven o'clock," she chirped. "I'll text you our home address in the next few minutes."

"Sounds good. What should I bring for dinner?"

"Nothing but that charming smile of yours. Ciao, Romeo. *A presto!*"

Ending the call, Romeo told his brother about their plans for the evening. "After the Christmas and Cocktails event

we're going to a dinner party at Davide and Aurora Bordellio's apartment."

Frowning, Enrique scratched at his square chin. "Who's
that?"

Romeo hesitated, considered his options. If he told Enrique about his traffic accident, he'd ream him out for being
distracted behind the wheel. Romeo wasn't in the mood
for one of his brother's lectures. Still, he had to tell him
something, and decided to come clean to his brother about
the accident, Zoe's unexpected arrival at his office hours
later, the *Amore in Tuscany* movie premiere, and the disastrous after-party at Milano Cocktail Bar starring Lizabeth.

"All of that happened in one day?" Enrique asked, an
awestruck expression on his face.

"Crazy, right?"

"Yeah, man, it is. And Zoe sounds like a spitfire. I
can't believe she ripped up a check for a hundred thousand euros, then threw it in your face. I'd take it, and I'm
your brother!"

Romeo picked up his cell, punched in his password and
accessed the pictures on his phone. Pleased with the photographs he'd taken with Zoe at the after-party, he showed
them to his brother. He then pulled up her FaceChat page
and read some of her previous posts.

Enrique whistled, and Romeo's chest puffed up with
pride.

"Gorgeous, right?" Romeo said, scrolling through the
photographs. "What a beauty."

Peering at the cell phone screen, Enrique tapped it with
an index finger. "According to Zoe's timeline, she won a
cycling competition in June, hiked the Alps with one of
her colleagues and is organizing a Christmas toy drive for
a Milan orphanage. That's impressive."

"I told you Zoe's the total package. She's everything a man could want, and more."

"Then what are you waiting for? Why haven't you wooed her with your wit and charm?"

Romeo blew out a deep breath. "Because she won't give me the time of day."

"Sucks to be you, huh?"

"Tell me about it. I still feel guilty about the accident, and tried to make amends by giving Zoe gifts and money, but she refused. She accused me of trying to buy her silence, and when I saw her at the fashion house on Monday afternoon, she was ice cold—"

"I don't blame her. You think the worst of people, especially women. The older you get, the more pessimistic you are about life."

"Do you blame me? Every woman I've ever dated has screwed me."

"Quit looking over your shoulder at the past," he admonished in a somber tone of voice. "Learn from the mistakes you made in your previous relationships, then move on. If you don't, you'll never have the love you deserve."

"You need to stop watching Telemundo novelas." Romeo couldn't keep a straight face and chuckled. "They're making you soft and dramatic as hell!"

Enrique chucked his empty beer can at Romeo, but he caught it with one hand, shot it toward the garbage and flashed a toothy grin when it dropped into the oversize bin.

"What are you going to do about Zoe? Come correct or give up?"

"Give up? Man, please." Romeo raised a hand to his mouth, blew on his fingernails, then rubbed them on the sleeve of his orange jersey. "Ambitious is my middle name."

"Cool, so you have a plan? Something big in the works to impress her?"

"Of course. I'm going to have flowers and Godiva chocolate delivered to her office tomorrow. When she calls to thank me I'll convince her to have dinner with me."

Enrique scoffed. "No offense, bro, but you send flowers and candy to everyone."

"Since you fancy yourself a love doctor, what do you propose I do?"

"Think outside the box. Do something different. Plan a date with her interests in mind," he advised. "What does Zoe like? What does she do on her days off? Who's her favorite band?"

Good question, Romeo thought, drumming his fingers on the picnic table. Reflecting on the conversation they'd had at Milano Cocktail Bar, he remembered how excited she'd been discussing her plans for the holidays.

Romeo coughed into his fist. Christmas was hard for him. Had been ever since his nephew Lucca had died. He couldn't look at a gingerbread house without remembering all the times he'd built one with his adorable five-year-old nephew. Romeo wanted to create new memories with Zoe.

Thinking about the holidays and all the fun events in and around the city, an idea took shape in his mind. *Why didn't I think of this sooner?* He'd plan a romantic date for Zoe, and soon she'd be singing his praises. "Thanks, bro. I know just what to do."

"Good. I'll send you my bill." Chuckling, Enrique picked up his cell, swiped his finger across the screen, then sighed in relief. "Thank God. Isabelle finally texted me back."

"We should get going," Romeo said, glancing at his smartwatch. "Christmas and Cocktails starts at five o'clock, which gives us thirty minutes to get ready, so let's bounce."

Enrique stood, grabbed his backpack and slung it over his shoulder. "Count me out."

"Why the sudden change of heart?" Romeo asked, rising to his feet.

"I need to bring my baby back home where she belongs. Isabelle's going to Dolce Vita Milan to celebrate a colleague's birthday. She'll be leaving the celebrity hotspot at the end of the night on *my* arm. There's no ifs, ands or buts about it."

Romeo clapped him on the shoulder. "What are you waiting for, bro? Go get your girl!"

Chapter 9

"Zoe, come here," Aurora called from inside her cozy, wallpapered kitchen. Dipping a serving spoon into the metal pot on the stainless steel stove, she stirred the home-made stew with gusto. "I need you to try this and tell me what you think it's missing."

Zoe glanced up from the CDs she was holding in her hands and stared at Aurora. *Why me?* she thought, her stomach churning in protest. *I hate tortellini stew.* Standing in front of the entertainment unit, riffling through Davide's enormous music collection, Zoe decided to temporarily put her search for a Christmas CD on hold and put the discs on the glass coffee table. "Sure, Aurora, no problem. I'll be right there."

Careful not to bump into anything, Zoe exited the living room. In walking distance of Casa Di Moda, the three-bedroom apartment had high ceilings and oversize windows that offered stunning views of the city center. Small but luxurious, it was packed with antique furniture, wooden sculptures and leafy plants. There were photographs everywhere—on the pale pink walls, on the bookshelves, along the kitchen countertops—and there were so many cushions on the couches, Zoe didn't know where to sit down.

The apartment reflected Casa Di Moda's exuberant prints and colors, and seeing the fashion house logo painted above the fireplace reminded Zoe of all the paperwork waiting for her on her office desk. Tomorrow, after her trip to the market with Jiovanni, she'd stop at the fashion house and finalize the details for the Men of Milan calendar. Zoe wanted everything to be perfect for the Christmas promotion and was pumped about the upcoming photo shoot.

"It smells delicious," Zoe lied, taking the spoon into her mouth and tasting the thick brown liquid. "It needs oregano if you have it."

Chuckling, Davide nodded his head in agreement. "I told her the exact same thing five minutes ago, but she didn't believe me. It's *my* mother's recipe. Go figure!"

"*Silenzo!*" Aurora yelled, swatting her husband's shoulder. "*So cosa sto facendo!*"

"If you know what you're doing then why does the tortellini taste like medicine?"

Aurora slapped his shoulder, and Davide gave a hearty laugh.

"You know you love me," he joked, wrapping his arms around his wife's trim waist.

"Not as much as you love yourself!"

Laughing, they snuggled against each other. Their display of affection made Zoe wish she had someone special in her life. Or at the very least, someone to hang out with on her days off. Zoe hugged her hands to her chest. It had been so long since she'd been intimate with a man she longed to be kissed and caressed.

Yeah, by Romeo Morretti! shouted her inner voice.

Swallowing hard, she cleared all thoughts of the bad-boy businessman from her mind. It didn't work. The more she tried to bury them, the stronger they were. Like on Monday. Romeo arrived at the office for a private tour, and when she'd bumped into him in the hallway, he'd surprised her with a hug and a kiss on each cheek. It was hard, but she'd kept her distance. Thankfully, she'd spoken to Lizabeth at the after-party and knew what his shtick was. How he got off on seducing women. Deep down, Zoe was flattered by his attention, but she wasn't going to waste her time with a man who'd never commit to her.

"Do you want me to set the table?" Zoe asked.

Davide shook his head. "I got it. You're in charge of the music, remember?"

"We're glad you're here," Aurora said. "It's going to be an amazing night. I can feel it."

Zoe spotted an empty wine bottle beside the toaster and suspected her boss was tipsy. She'd called to invite her over for dinner that afternoon, so Zoe could bring her up to speed about the Casa Di Moda photo shoot in Florence yesterday, and since Jiovanni was busy with his new lady love, Alessandra Esposito, she'd gladly accepted. Spending another Saturday night alone was depressing, and Zoe would rather hang out with her boss than watch TV or journal about her week.

Or so she'd thought.

From the moment Zoe arrived at the apartment the couple had been grilling her about her love life. She'd quickly changed the subject, had chatted excitedly about the overwhelming online response to the pictures she'd posted on Casa Di Moda's website from the Florence photoshoot. Soon the couple was helping her brainstorm ideas for the holiday campaign.

The doorbell rang, and Aurora hopped around the

kitchen like a rabbit in a meadow. "Honey, hurry, it's seven o'clock. Set the table, light some candles and select the wine!" Aurora shrieked. "Zoe, would you be a dear and answer the door? As you can see our hands are full, and I don't want to keep our guest waiting."

Zoe didn't know what the fuss was about, didn't understand why Aurora and Davide were suddenly speaking to each other in hushed tones. She'd had dinner at the Bordellio house before, and although Aurora complained about her mother-in-law being impossible to please, Zoe liked the retired college professor. She loved hearing her hilarious stories about former students. "Not a problem at all."

Not wanting the elderly woman to wait, Zoe rushed into the foyer and opened the front door. Her mouth opened, then closed, and her knees wobbled under her striped sweaterdress. Zoe knew she was staring at Romeo, but she couldn't help it. Couldn't take her eyes off him.

"Good evening, Zoe. It's great to see you again."

The sound of his voice jolted Zoe back to the present. "What are you doing here?" she blurted out.

"I'm here for Davide and Aurora's dinner party, of course."

"What dinner party? I'm the only one here."

Romeo licked his lips, and desire rippled across Zoe's clammy skin.

"Great, so I won't have to compete with anyone else for your attention," he said, his deep brown eyes dark with mischief. "I can have you all to myself tonight. How wonderful."

Flabbergasted, Zoe couldn't think of anything to say in response and fidgeted with her hands. It was either that or use them to caress his broad chest. God help her. Dark and brooding, with a smoldering gaze, she couldn't help checking him out.

Narrowing her eyes, she noticed the unique style and fit of his tan sports coat. It was one of Casa Di Moda's bestsellers, and that morning Zoe had mentioned it on the fashion house's social media pages. Stylishly dressed, he'd paired it with a ribbed flex-collar shirt, slim-fit pants and leather shoes. One look turned her on, but she had to keep her head, knew she couldn't fall victim to his piercing gaze. Like all of the women in his past, she was nothing more than a challenge to him. She deserved more than a one-night stand with a bad-boy bachelor.

"How do you do it?"

Blinking, Zoe wore a blank expression on her face. "Do what?"

"Manage to look more beautiful every time I see you." Leaning forward, he kissed her on each cheek, then took her hand in his. "I'm glad you're here, Zoe. I've missed you."

"Missed me? You don't even know me."

"Not yet, but I'm working on it. In my defense, you're not making it easy for me."

Romeo winked at her. He looked pleased with himself, and the expression on his face made a giggle tickle her throat. Damn him! He was suave and flirtatious, and knew how to make her laugh. His boyish smile and his scent aroused her body.

Soft music filled the apartment, creating a romantic mood. The air smelled of spices and freshly baked garlic bread. Zoe wondered what else Aurora and Davide were cooking up. She loved them, but she didn't appreciate them tricking her.

"Romeo, you made it. Welcome to our humble abode."

Davide appeared in the foyer, grinning from ear to ear.

"Thanks for having me. It's great to be here," he said politely.

"Come in. Aurora's just finishing up in the kitchen. She'll join us shortly."

"This is for you and your lovely wife."

For the first time, Zoe noticed Romeo was holding a gift

bag. Davide opened it and nodded in appreciation at the bottle of Cristal. Listening to the men make small talk, questions rose in Zoe's mind. Was Romeo the only guest? Had they invited other potential investors? Was she expected to help the couple close the deal? There was only one way to find out.

Excusing herself, Zoe marched down the hall, intent on speaking to Aurora before dinner. She spotted Aurora standing in front of the sink and sprang into action. Gripping her shoulders, she steered her into the walk-in pantry and closed the door.

"What are you doing? I have to take the vegetables off the stove or they'll be soggy."

"Dinner can wait," she said, folding her arms across her chest. "You lied to me."

Making her eyes wide, Aurora wore an innocent smile. "No I didn't."

"Why didn't you tell me you invited Romeo to dinner?"

"Because if I told you he was coming tonight you wouldn't have shown up and I need you. You're my good-luck charm."

"Why is he here? Is this a business dinner? Have you invited other potential investors?"

"We don't need anyone else," Aurora said. "Romeo can single-handedly save Casa Di Moda, so be nice to him tonight, okay? Flirt with him, laugh at his jokes and quit playing hard to get. Guys hate that, especially wealthy men."

Zoe didn't speak for a long moment. She couldn't. Didn't know how to react to her boss's statement, and feared if she spoke, she'd lose her temper. Was Aurora drunk? High on seasoning salt and garlic? *She's crazy if she thinks I'm going to sleep with Romeo to save Casa Di Moda from bankruptcy. As if. I'm a public relations director, not a whore.*

"Italian men like bold, assertive women. Don't be afraid to make the first move," Aurora advised. "He's quite the catch, Zoe…"

I know, she thought sourly. *How can I forget? You keep reminding me!*

"Invite Romeo back to your place at the end of the night, toast your newfound friendship with an expensive bottle of wine and do what comes naturally. I would!"

"Are you suggesting I sleep with Romeo Morretti to save Casa Di Moda?"

Aurora scoffed, wore a skeptical expression on her heart-shaped face. "As if you don't want to. He's hot, successful and ridiculously rich. What more could you want in a man?"

What more indeed? Biting her bottom lip, Zoe dodged her boss's gaze.

"Exactly. That's what I thought. You want him, so stop fighting your attraction."

"I've never had a one-night stand—"

"Who says it has to be just one night?" Aurora asked, raising an eyebrow. "You have the entire weekend to explore the mysterious wonders of Romeo Morretti."

"I can't. That's not me. Sex without love is meaningless."

"Says who? I sowed my wild oats before I married Davide, and I'm glad I did. How are you supposed to know what you like sexually if you don't date a variety of men? Hooking up with Romeo Morretti is a once-in-a-lifetime opportunity. Don't blow it."

"Don't blow it?" Zoe repeated. "If you want Romeo to invest in Casa Di Moda so bad, then *you* sleep with him."

"He doesn't want me. He wants you."

Opening her mouth, she realized she didn't know what to say, and closed it.

"You have to help us," Aurora begged, clasping her hands together. "Romeo's not only insanely popular, he also has billionaire friends with deep pockets. If he throws his support behind Casa Di Moda, we'll finally make it to the top."

Hearing voices in the kitchen, Zoe pressed a finger to

her mouth to silence her boss. She didn't want Davide or Romeo to overhear them, or worse, figure out they were hiding in the pantry and come looking for them. How embarrassing, she thought, expelling a deep breath.

Zoe looked down at her outfit and scrunched up her nose. Her dress was cute, just not snazzy enough to have dinner with the sexiest man on the planet. If she'd known Romeo was coming, she would have done her hair and makeup and worn something fancy.

Hoping the coast was clear, Zoe cracked open the door and peered out to the kitchen. Thankfully, Romeo and Davide were in the living room, watching football on the flat-screen TV mounted above the fireplace. "The coast is clear."

"Let's go. It's time to wow our millionaire guest," Aurora whispered, tiptoeing out of the pantry. "Remember what I said. Be warm and friendly and flirt like crazy."

Zoe didn't know whether to laugh or to cry.

"Romeo, how nice for you to join us for dinner. You're looking well…"

Standing, Romeo greeted Aurora, but his gaze was glued to Zoe's face. The Casa Di Moda logo was visible on the pocket of his dress shirt, confirming her initial thought. Romeo was trying to impress her, and she liked seeing him in her favorite designer label.

God help her. He was across the room, but her attraction to him was so strong her body trembled at the sight of him. Zoe pulled herself together. Refused to crumble under pressure. She could do this. It didn't matter that Romeo was all man, all muscle. Zoe had a job to do, and although she disagreed with Aurora's strategy, she was going to help her boss save Casa Di Moda—even though it meant befriending a man who made her weak in the knees.

Chapter 10

Romeo picked up his glass, noticed Zoe watching him from across the dining room table and met her gaze. He read the question in her eyes and smiled to reassure her he didn't bite. That he'd never do anything to embarrass her in front of her boss. Arriving at the Bordellio apartment an hour earlier, he'd discovered Zoe didn't know he'd been invited to dinner, so he'd made small talk with Davide and given her some space.

Sitting back comfortably in his chair, he sipped his drink and savored the sweet, fruity taste. Romeo wished he had something stronger to drink than orange iced tea, but his doctor wanted him to limit his alcohol intake, and he didn't want to do anything to jeopardize his health.

"Would anyone like more chicken cacciatore?" Aurora asked, gesturing to the round ceramic bowl beside the bottle of Cristal he'd brought for the couple as a gift. "Don't be shy. There's a lot more food in the kitchen, so eat up."

Before Romeo could decline, Aurora scooped more pasta onto his plate, and enough sautéed vegetables to feed a family of five. *"Godere!"*

Romeo gulped. His stomach groaned in protest at the thought of eating more food, but he smiled at his eager-to-please host. Italian women took cooking very seriously, and since he didn't want to offend the fashion designer he said, "Thank you, Aurora."

Pride shimmered in her eyes, but she gave a dismissive wave of her hand, as if whipping up a seven-course meal on her day off was no big deal. "It's my pleasure. I love cooking. If I weren't a fashion designer, I'd probably own an Italian restaurant."

Romeo nodded. That explained the extravagant meal and romantic ambience in the dining room. The lights were low, classical music was playing on the stereo system, and rose petals bordered the swan-themed centerpiece. Scented candles perfumed the air with a floral fragrance. Romeo wondered if Aurora was a serial matchmaker who got a kick out of setting people up. Or had she invited him over tonight to persuade him to invest in Casa Di Moda? Romeo was used to people wanting things from him—loans they had no intention of repaying, managerial positions within his company even though they weren't qualified, a meeting with one of his brothers or cousins—but he hoped for Zoe's sake that Aurora wasn't using her as bait.

His brother's words came back to him, filling him with guilt. *You think the worst of people, and the older you get, the more pessimistic you are about life and relationships.* Enrique was right, but it wasn't his fault. Friends and lovers had burned him too many times to count. After everything Lizabeth had put him through, he'd shut himself off to the world. Had stopped giving interviews to the media.

Quit attending social functions and events. Kept the opposite sex at arm's length.

Then why are you sweating Zoe Smith? his inner voice broke into his thoughts. *Why are you pursuing a woman who doesn't want to date you?*

Romeo sighed. It was a good question. One he didn't have an answer to, but wished he did. Her natural beauty had caught his eye. It was what drew him to her that fateful morning. But after attending the movie premiere with her and the after-party, Romeo knew Zoe was more than just a pretty face with God-given curves. Women with a sense of humor who weren't afraid to laugh at themselves always impressed him. He enjoyed the PR director's killer wit. These days, everyone was sensitive about everything, but Zoe wasn't afraid to speak her mind. It was a turn-on, what made him want to be around her, even though she was playing hard to get.

Again, his inner voice mocked him. *Who says she's playing?*

Romeo picked up his fork and forced himself to finish the food. The chicken was dry, the vegetables were overcooked, but he acted as if it were the best meal he'd ever had. It was a small price to pay for spending the night with the object of his affection. Zoe was quiet, only gave one-word responses to his questions, but Romeo wasn't discouraged. He had two concert tickets in his wallet, and Zoe was going to jump for joy when she found out he was taking her to see her favorite group in December.

"Zoe, tell me more about your day trip to Florence."

"Yes," Davide agreed. "Fill us in on the photo shoot in my beloved hometown."

Clearing her throat, she fiddled with her napkin and shifted nervously in her chair.

To put her at ease, Romeo touched her hand, giving it

a light squeeze. Electricity singed his skin. Feeling her soft flesh against his caused his mouth to dry and desire to shoot through his veins. "Was the weather nice, or was it gray and rainy as usual?"

Lines wrinkled her forehead. "How did you know I was in Florence yesterday?"

"Social media, of course."

Freeing her hand from his grasp, Zoe picked up her glass and took a long drink.

"By the way, your post about the Duomo was spot-on. You're right. The city should do something about the pigeons and those sleazy scam artists loitering outside the Duomo cathedral. They're rude and aggressive, and they drive tourists away."

Her face brightened. "I agree. It's a terrible situation. Those scam artists give Milan a bad name. Something *has* to be done about them."

"If you ever decide to run for city council, you have my vote!"

Zoe giggled. Romeo knew if he kept her talking and laughing about the things she was passionate about they'd be friends—and lovers—in no time.

"Florence was lovely." Her shoulders visibly relaxed, her tone filled with excitement. "The weather was warm and sunny, the crew was fantastic, and we had so much fun sightseeing, Jiovanni promised we'd go back next month for the tree-lighting ceremony."

Romeo almost fell off his chair. Zoe had a man? Since when? As he spoke, he tried to maintain his cool, but he heard the bass in his voice and wanted to kick himself for sounding jealous. "Jiovanni? Who's that? Your boyfriend?"

Aurora burst out laughing, and even though Zoe glared at her, she didn't stop giggling.

"He's not her boyfriend. He's an associate designer at Casa Di Moda," Aurora said.

Romeo sighed in relief, thanking his lucky stars that Zoe wasn't spoken for.

"Zoe's interested in someone else, and it isn't her BFF Jiovanni. He's a successful businessman who knows how to treat a woman. Isn't that right, Zoe?"

Eyes narrowed, lips pursed, Zoe gripped her fork in her hands. If looks could kill Aurora would be slumped over her plate, dead. But the designer was so busy chatting a mile a minute she didn't notice the murderous expression on Zoe's face.

Recognizing the tension in the air, Davide wisely changed the subject. He made everyone around the table chuckle when he poked fun at himself for eating so much food one of the buttons popped off his dress shirt. As they ate dinner, the mood lightened and conversation flowed. They discussed their plans for the holidays, their favorite traditions and Christmas events in Milan. Two glasses of Cristal helped Zoe loosen up, and by the time the group retired to the living room, she was in great spirits. She spoke Italian well, even knew slang and cultural jokes. The sound of her voice speaking his native tongue with such confidence and eloquence was a turn-on. A deep thinker who loved to discuss and debate current events, he was completely and utterly captivated by her.

"Have you had an opportunity to review the business proposal I gave you on Monday?" Davide asked, setting his mug down on the coffee table. "I know it's only been a few days since you visited Casa Di Moda, but I'd love to know your initial thoughts on the proposal."

Romeo wiped his mouth with a silk napkin. "Thanks again for having me. It was great to have a behind-the-scenes look at a successful fashion house. I learned a lot about the day-to-day operations of your company. I read your business proposal, and although it was concise and well-written, I'm not prepared to invest in Casa Di Moda at this time."

Davide nodded, and Aurora hung her head.

"We understand. Thanks for taking the time to read the proposal. We appreciate it."

"Davide, all isn't lost." To lighten the mood, Romeo spoke in a jovial tone of voice. "I mentioned the proposal to my sister, Francesca, yesterday and she expressed interest in the line. However, she was disappointed in the size chart—"

"Oh," Aurora said, interrupting him. "Why would your sister be disappointed in our size chart?"

"Francesca isn't a size two. She's a tall, voluptuous woman who has trouble finding designer clothes that fit her shape. If you want her to consider investing in Casa Di Moda, you'll have to revise your size chart."

Aurora's face paled. Her mouth was open so wide Romeo could see her molars.

"Casa Di Moda makes beautiful, fashionable clothes for *all* women," Zoe explained, leaning forward in her armchair, her smile as captivating as her sultry voice. "Our Christmas ad campaign features models of all colors, shapes and sizes, but what we're most excited about this holiday season is unveiling our new Chic and Curvy line."

Davide coughed into his fist, then an awkward silence descended over the room.

What was *that* about? The couple was fidgeting and shifting around on the love seat, but Zoe looked pumped up, as if she were bursting with good news. Frowning, Romeo tried to recall what he'd read in the proposal Davide had given him days earlier. Swamped all week at the office, he'd reviewed so many documents and contracts that facts and statistics were swimming around in his head. "Really? I didn't know Casa Di Moda was in the process of expanding its line. That wasn't mentioned in the proposal."

Aurora and Davide stared at each other, their expressions glum.

"Why don't I send over some sample dresses for your sister to check out?" Zoe proposed, flipping her braids over her shoulders. "If Francesca loves them, which I *know* she will, we can set up a meeting to discuss investment possibilities. How does that sound?"

"Zoe, that would be great," he said with a broad smile. "How generous of you."

Aurora shot to her feet as if the couch were on fire. Zoe offered to help her clear the table, but the fashion designer wouldn't hear of it. "No, no, be a good guest and visit with Romeo while Davide and I prepare dessert."

Leaving the room, the couple smiled politely, but Romeo could tell by their demeanor that they were upset. Were they angry about Zoe's offer? Did they have a problem with the PR director giving away free samples of their clothes? Was Zoe in trouble? He suspected Casa Di Moda wasn't the big, happy family they wanted him to believe it was, but decided not to share his suspicions with his sister. If he did, it would sour her opinion of the fashion house, and possibly even Zoe, and Romeo couldn't risk that happening. Zoe was warming up to him, he could feel it, sensed it in her cheeky grin and easy laugh, and he didn't want to do anything to rock the boat. Not when she'd finally let down her guard.

Pleased to have Zoe to himself, he draped an arm around the back of the couch. "When I tell Francesca about your offer she's going to be your new BFF. My sister loves free clothes."

"Every girl does. Buying a woman a fabulous dress is the quickest way to win her heart."

Romeo made his eyes wide. "Really? Francesca told me it was diamonds!"

"Not for me. Expensive jewelry isn't my thing—"

"What about concert tickets? Would that win you over?"

"It depends." Zoe plucked a piece of cheese off the silver tray and chewed it. "I'd be totally stoked to see Adele, Mariah, or Il Divo. They're an outstanding group, and I'm their biggest fan."

"Ask and ye shall receive." Romeo reached into this pocket and took out the tickets. "I hope you don't have plans on December thirteenth, because it's Il Divo night."

Zoe plucked the tickets out of his hand and studied them as if she were committing the details to memory. "This can't be real. I must be dreaming."

Amused by her reaction, Romeo studied her, his smile growing by the second.

"T-T-These are front-row seats," she stammered. "One ticket is two thousand euros. I don't have that kind of money. It would take me months to pay you back."

"Zoe, we're going on a date. It won't cost you anything."

Worry lines wrinkled her smooth brow.

"I don't know if you've noticed, but I'm very good at what I do, and I make a decent living at Morretti Finance and Investments."

Dodging his gaze, she dropped the tickets on the table and shook her head.

"Don't frown." Angling his body, he moved closer to her on the couch. "When you do, the light in your eyes fades, and your smile loses its warmth."

"I can't go with you to the concert. It's not a good idea."

"Why not? I think you're dope, and I want to date you—"

A smirk curled her lips, distracting him, and Romeo trailed off speaking.

"Dope?" she repeated, the humor evident in her tone of voice. "What is it, 1995? Where's your boom box, your white Adidas kicks and your gold chains?"

Romeo gave a hearty chuckle. He didn't mind her poking fun at him, could feel the tension in the air recede as they chatted and laughed together. The instrumental version of the song "This Christmas" was playing on the stereo system, and Zoe sang the words as she gazed out the windows. Lights twinkled in the distance, showering the night sky with brilliant colors. The music added to the peaceful ambience.

"Why do you keep turning me down? I'm starting to think you don't like me, but what's not to like?" he joked, playfully popping his shirt collar. "I'm a good old-fashioned Italian boy who's chivalrous, ambitious and passionate about life—"

"Yes, I've heard. You *certainly* get around."

Her words gave him pause. Now he understood why Zoe was keeping him at a distance, and decided to put her fears to rest. He didn't talk about his past relationship with anyone except his family, but he felt compelled to open up to Zoe. Didn't want her to think he was a lying dog who mistreated women. He wanted her to know the truth about his past, come what may.

"Have I been a Boy Scout? No. Have I dated more than one woman at a time? Yes. Would I settle down and quit playing the field if I met the right woman? Absolutely." Romeo raised an index finger in the air. "One date. That's all I'm asking. Come on, Zoe. Don't make me beg."

"Why me?" she asked, folding her arms across her chest. "There are tons of women who'd kill to go to the Il Divo concert with you, so why are you sweating me?"

"Sweating you? Is that what you think I'm doing?"

"If the shoe fits…" she said, her voice fading into silence.

Romeo glanced over his shoulder. He heard cupboards slam, high heels smacking against the hardwood floors and strident voices coming from the kitchen. The Bordellios were angry about something, but what?

"Don't take this the wrong way, but we're all wrong for each other. I'm ready to settle down and start a family, and you're busy playing the field."

Her words bothered him, made him regret his partying, boozing ways in the past. But he didn't interrupt, listening as she spoke from the heart.

"Furthermore, Lizabeth told me you're trying to work things out, and I don't want to come between you. I'm not a home-wrecker, and I don't want to be labeled one."

"She said *what*?"

"That you're still madly in love and committed to each other."

Romeo scoffed. *The only thing Lizabeth is committed to is my checkbook!*

He gritted his teeth. His pulse was racing, his heart beating so fast he feared he needed immediate medical attention. It took supreme effort, but Romeo took a deep breath and spoke in a calm voice. "That's not true. None of it is. We broke up over a year ago, and I've moved on with my life." He added, "I wish she'd do the same."

Hope sparked in her big brown eyes. "So, you're not getting back together?"

"Absolutely not. We're through, and there's nothing she could say or do to change my mind."

"Why would Lizabeth lie to me?"

"Because she knows I'm interested in you."

"Romeo, quit saying that. You know nothing about me."

"Of course I do. You're an avid cyclist who loves swimming, traveling, journaling and pop music," he said, proud of himself for taking the time to check out her social media pages when he'd returned home from the park that afternoon. "You're a self-proclaimed shopaholic who's always on the lookout for a unique find and a great bargain."

"You did your homework. I'm impressed."

Zoe wore a pensive expression on her face. He suspected she was contemplating whether or not to go with him to the Il Divo concert. This was a first. He'd met women from all walks of life, from executives to heiresses and international pop stars, but he'd never had to work so hard to convince someone to go on a date with him.

"Over the summer, you were linked to several celebrities in the tabloids. You expect me to believe you're not hooking up with any of them?"

His eyebrows shot up. Romeo wasn't used to being asked point-blank questions about his relationship status. He was taken aback by Zoe's boldness and disappointed by her skepticism. Why didn't she believe him? What did he have to do to prove that he wasn't the heartless Casanova the media made him out to be?

"I'm going to be honest, Romeo. I like you, and I want to get to know you better, but not if you're stringing other women along or playing the field."

"I'm not, so please don't judge me by my past mistakes. Accept me for who I am today, a sincere, trustworthy man who's so damn sexy you can't stop staring at me."

Zoe giggled, and the sound of her loud, high-pitched laugh made Romeo so happy he did the unthinkable... He crushed his lips to her mouth.

Chapter 11

Romeo devoured Zoe's moist, plump lips. Consumed with desire, he savored the taste of her sweet mouth. Flavored with hints of wine and spices, her lips were delicious. Addictive. Stronger than any drug, and Romeo was hooked. He kissed her slowly, softly, with such tender loving care she moaned inside his mouth. As if she were starving and he was dinner. *Have it your way!* he thought, inhaling her fragrant scent. *I'm all in, and eager to please!*

Lost in the moment, he stroked her cheeks, her neck, her shoulders, took great pleasure in caressing her smooth flesh. Her scent consumed him, gave him a rush. He'd never desired a woman more, and could think of nothing better than holding Zoe in his arms for the rest of the night. It took every ounce of self-control he had not to slide his hands under her fitted dress.

"That was nice," he whispered, nibbling on her bottom lip. "Hashtag, best kiss ever."

Her face lit up, and a girlish smile warmed her lips. "You're right. That was some kiss."

Romeo brushed his nose against her cheek, and she purred in his ear. That was all the encouragement he needed. Closing his eyes, he pressed his mouth against hers again. This time, her shoulders didn't stiffen. She touched his cheek with her palm and gently stroked his skin. Romeo wanted to cheer. To pump his fist in the air. She was warming up to him, and that was reason to celebrate. And they would at the Il Divo concert. Thoughts and ideas crowded his mind, but Romeo pushed them aside. In that moment all that mattered was pleasing Zoe, and he needed to focus on the task at hand.

Her tongue tickled his, sending shivers careening down his spine. He caressed her cheek with his thumb, enjoyed the feel of her skin. Romeo hadn't planned on making a move, and never imagined their first kiss would be in her boss's living room, but he had no regrets.

"What are you doing?" she murmured against his mouth.

"Living in the moment."

Romeo reached out and touched her hair, slowly sliding a braid between his fingers.

"I haven't been able to stop thinking about you since the day we met," he confessed, brushing his mouth against hers. "Since nothing would make me happier than taking you to the Il Divo concert, give me an early Christmas present and agree to be my date."

"How can I refuse when you asked me so nicely? *Several* times."

Romeo had nothing to lose and craved the taste of her lips again, so he kissed her passionately with everything he had. To his surprise, Zoe, draped her arms around his neck and pressed her body flat against his. Panting, she explored his mouth, searching, teasing, turning him out with each flick of her tongue. Falling victim to the lust of his flesh, he slipped a hand under her dress and caressed her thighs. Romeo knew he was crossing the line, but he couldn't stop stroking her warm skin. "The Il Divo concert is going to be epic," he whispered.

"Epic, huh? Tell me more."

"And ruin the surprise? *Non c'è modo.*"

"No way?" Her lips flared into a pout. "Keep talking like that, Mr. Man, and you'll be going to the Il Divo concert *alone.*"

"You're bluffing. You're so excited about the concert, I bet it's all you can think about."

A grin curled her lips as she spoke to him in Italian.

Romeo liked hearing Zoe speak Italian. Her low, sultry voice was his undoing. His Kryptonite. What pushed him over the edge. He couldn't resist. Couldn't stop himself from kissing her over and over again, until he couldn't catch his breath and had to come up for air. "You have incredible eyes and the most amazing lips."

"Is that right? And how many women have you used that line on?"

"Just once. I wanted homemade ciabatta, and my nonna refused, so I told her she was the most beautiful woman to ever walk the face of the earth. It worked like a charm."

Romeo heard his cell phone buzzing from inside his back pocket but ignored it, focusing his attention on Zoe and nothing else. To make her laugh, he joked, "You're all that and a bag of chips…and a Kit Kat!"

Zoe cracked up. "You must have been a nineties rapper in another life, because you have the lingo down pat."

"It's not my fault. My older brothers used to love American hip-hop when I was a kid. It was all they listened to," he explained, as fond memories came to mind. "We used to have rap battles every day, so I can spit rhymes with the best of them."

Something crashed to the floor in the kitchen, and Romeo glanced over his shoulder. Zoe said, "I'm going to check on Aurora and Davide."

"Oh, no you're not." Romeo seized Zoe's hand, forcing her to sit back down on the couch, and entwined his fingers with hers. "You're not going anywhere. You're kicking it with me."

Romeo took his cell out of his pocket, punched in his password and noticed he had several new text messages from Giuseppe and his COO, Simona Vitti. His publicist wanted to meet with him on Monday morning to discuss various social events happening during the holiday season. Romeo was looking forward to touching base with him. He wanted to spend the Christmas holidays with Zoe and was eager to show her off to his friends and family.

Reading the text from Simona caused a frown to curl his lips.

Call me back tonight. It doesn't matter how late. We need to talk about the deal with Milan Breweries Limited. I have some concerns, and I need to discuss them with you.

Beads of sweat formed on his forehead. Was the million-dollar deal in jeopardy? Were there legal issues? Did the rest of his executive team have reservations, too, or just Simona? Romeo wanted to return her call, but decided to wait until he left the Bordellio apartment. Zoe was opening to him, and he didn't want to ruin the mood by talking on the phone with his staff. He composed a message to Simona, promising to call her in an hour, then hit the send button.

"You're a popular guy," Zoe said, her eyebrows raised in a questioning slant.

"I'm sorry. It's work. This will only take a minute."

"Romeo, relax. I'm joking. Take as long as you need."

As Romeo responded to his text messages, he enjoyed listening to Zoe sing along with the Andrea Bocelli CD playing on the stereo system. Her voice was strong and clear, full of emotion. As she belted out the lyrics to "I'll Be Home for Christmas," he realized she was a woman of many talents. Finished, he handed Zoe his cell and draped an arm around her waist. "Enter your birthdate on my calendar, because I go all out for women who smell like heaven, sing like angels and look like centerfolds."

"Are you *sure* you're an investment banker and not in show business?"

"If that's your way of telling me I'm the bomb, I agree. I am. Just ask my nonna!"

Zoe pressed her lips together, and Romeo could tell she was trying not to laugh.

"I bet you were a handful in elementary school," she said, with a knowing smile. "You probably had girls fighting over you and pledging their undying love on the playground."

"I didn't, but my brothers did. I was a scrawny kid who had no friends and no game."

Zoe wore a thoughtful expression on her face. "I know how you feel. I was socially awkward, too, and being the tallest person in my class made me an easy target for bullies. If not for my best friend, I never would have survived."

They sat in silence for several moments, listening to the music.

"I like this. Us hanging out. We should do it more often." Watching her type her contact information into his cell, Romeo wished her hands were on him instead of his phone. "Let's have dinner tomorrow night. Pick a time and place and I'm there."

"Sorry, Romeo, but I have plans with Jiovanni."

"Are you free on Monday for *aperitivo*? We can have drinks at Bar Basso at seven o'clock." *Aperitivo* was a way of life in Milan, much like happy hour, it was an excuse for friends, colleagues and business associates to socialize and drink.

"I'll check my planner and get back to you."

Romeo nodded as if it was all good, but a plan was taking shape in his mind. If he didn't hear from her tomorrow he'd drop by Casa Di Moda on Monday and take her out for lunch.

"All done," Zoe said, handing over his cell phone. "Here you go."

When he took it from her, their fingers touched and all Romeo could think about was kissing her again.

Zoe started to speak, but it was Aurora's voice that filled the air.

"How wonderful! I *knew* you two would hit it off. You're a perfect match…"

I couldn't agree more. I've never been this enamored with a woman.

"I brought dessert." Entering the living room holding a silver tray, Aurora wore a bright smile.

"Nothing for me, thanks." Romeo discreetly glanced at his watch. "I had a great time tonight, but I should get going. I have a full day ahead of me tomorrow, and several important meetings."

"But it's Sunday," Zoe pointed out. "You need a day off just like everyone else."

No, he argued, his gaze glued to her lips. *I need to have you back in my arms so we can finish where we left off.*

"You're a man, Romeo, not a machine," she continued.

"I can relax when I retire. Until then, I have clients to impress, deals to close and money to make. It's a tough job, but somebody's gotta do it. I'm glad it's me." Standing, he offered Zoe his right hand. "I'll take you home."

"No, thank you. I'd like to speak to Aurora privately, so I'll call a cab when I'm ready to go."

Romeo was disappointed, but he nodded his head in understanding. Thanking the couple for their hospitality, he shook hands with Davide and kissed Aurora on the cheek.

"Don't be a stranger," Aurora said in a stern voice, though her eyes were smiling. "Next time you come over for dinner, bring your sister. We'd love to meet her."

In the foyer, Davide retrieved Romeo's coat from the closet and handed it to him.

Putting it on, he noticed Zoe standing beside the bookshelf. She waved, and for the second time in minutes, Romeo lost the battle with his flesh. He marched toward her and took her in his arms. Wanting to prove how he felt about her—even though the Bordellios were looking on— he kissed her soft, sweet mouth. Romeo wanted to pick up where they'd left off on the couch, but he felt the tension in her upper body and didn't want to upset her. Scared he was going to lose control, he whispered, *"Buona notte, bellissima,"* against her mouth, then turned and strode out the door.

Chapter 12

Thick gray clouds floated across the December sky, and the air smelled of rain, but there was nowhere else Zoe would rather be than biking through the streets of Milan with Jiovanni. The gloomy weather didn't detract from the beauty of her surroundings, and feeling the wind against her face had a calming effect on her. Every Sunday after morning Mass at the basilica Santa Maria delle Grazie, they'd bike to a nearby bistro to have brunch, then peruse the local flea markets. They'd shopped at booths selling seasonal crafts and traditional winter food and chatted with the vendors about their unique Christmas wares. It was the official start of the holiday season, and the towering cypress trees decorated in colored lights made the city look festive.

"Fifty years ago the rich were 'forced' to shop abroad in cities like Paris and London, but not anymore," Jiovanni explained, gripping the handlebars of his orange all-terrain bike. "I love fashion, but I liked it better when Milan had more green space and fewer boutiques…"

Listening with rapt attention, Zoe soaked up every word he said. Thanks to Jiovanni, she'd not only learned her way around Milan in a few short weeks, she'd also discovered interesting facts about Italy's most fashionable and sophisticated city. He pointed out ancient ruins, educated her about the significance of the architecture and offered valuable insights about living in the bustling metropolitan city. There was more to Milan than just fine cuisine and haute couture, and Zoe enjoyed Jiovanni's stories about the "good old days."

Pumping her brakes, Zoe swerved to avoid hitting a toddler who'd broken away from his family and darted in front of her bike. Milanese locals strolled about, hustling up and down the cobblestoned streets, laughing, snapping selfies and eating gelato.

Admiring the skyscrapers, the modern buildings and the attractive couples streaming in and out of restaurants and bars, Zoe soaked up the atmosphere of the city, the sounds of life and happiness swirling around her.

In the distance, Zoe spotted a wedding party posing for pictures in front of the Duomo and smiled. She loved weddings, and she couldn't take her eyes off the glowing couple hugging in front of the cathedral. They kissed for the cameras, and the sight warmed her heart. *Soon it will be my turn,* she thought. *I'll meet Mr. Right, he'll sweep me off my feet, and we'll spend the rest of our lives loving each other.*

An image of Romeo filled her thoughts. The memory of their first kiss burned bright in her mind. Played over and over again. That wasn't the worst of it. Feeling tipsy and flirtatious after several glasses of wine, she'd agreed to be his date for the Il Divo concert, but now she had second thoughts. Should she cancel? Should she go, but keep her distance?

Keep your distance? As if! responded her inner voice. *You were all over Romeo last night!*

Thinking about their impromptu make-out session in Aurora and Davide's living room caused goose bumps to break out. Romeo was unlike anyone she'd ever met, and being with him gave her a rush. They came from two different worlds, but she was curious about Romeo and his large, close-knit family. To her surprise, there was nothing cocky about him. They'd had so much fun at Aurora and Davide's apartment, Zoe was confident they'd have a good time at the Il Divo concert.

Slowing down so their bikes were side by side, Jiovanni led her through the crowded streets, around pedestrians weighed down with glitzy shopping bags and the luxury cars idling in front of stores. He suggested activities for them to do, but Zoe didn't feel like heading across town to Jiovanni's favorite museum. They'd been outside for hours, and just the thought of biking for another ninety minutes made her legs weak.

"*Evasione* is playing at Cinema Centrale at three o'clock." Jiovanni consulted his gold wristwatch. "That gives us an hour to get there. We better hurry, or we won't get seats."

"Or we could stop and have a snack at Goloso di Dolci," she proposed, her mouth watering at the thought of a sweet treat. "I'd love a cup of coffee and some gelato."

Jiovanni pointed across the street at the popular café on the corner. Famous for its unique flavors, fresh ingredients and generous servings, the ice cream shop was beloved by locals. "Count me out. There's a line around the block to get in."

"Okay. No worries," she said with a smile and a wave. "I'll see you tomorrow at work."

"All right, all right, quit twisting my arm. I'm coming."

Zoe smirked. "Of course you are. You love Goloso di Dolci more than I do!"

Stopping at the intersection, they got off their bikes, locked them to a lamppost swathed in garland, and jogged across the street. Joining the slow-moving line, Zoe took out her cell and checked her email. Her parents wanted her to call home, Shelby had sent dozens of pictures of her new Long Island apartment, and Aurora ranted about the full-figured line.

Get over it already! she thought, rolling her eyes. Zoe didn't understand why Aurora was being difficult. Last night, after Romeo left, Davide had thanked her profusely for pitching the Chic and Curvy line and assured her they'd vigorously promote it. He even agreed to a photo shoot in Naples next Friday, so why was Aurora being negative?

"I heard about the stunt you pulled last night at Aurora and Davide's apartment," Jiovanni said with a knowing smile. "You have huge cojones."

Stunned, Zoe glanced up from her cell phone, her mouth agape. Aurora had sworn her to secrecy about the dinner party, and even though she was dying to tell Jiovanni about Romeo and their magical first kiss, she'd respected her boss's wishes.

"I know a lot of gutsy women, but you're in a league of your own. You said you were going to do everything in your power to help Casa Di Moda succeed, and you meant it." Jiovanni saluted. "All hail the queen."

Zoe didn't laugh. "Who told you about the dinner party?"

"Lady Aurora, of course. She called me during lunch

while I was in the men's room and cursed me out for filling your head with outrageous ideas."

"Why didn't you say anything when you returned to the table?"

"Because you were flirting with the owner and I didn't want to ruin the mood!"

Zoe stuck out her tongue. "I was not flirting. You're just jealous because he comped my lunch."

"Guilty as charged. I hate seeing you with other men. You're my future wife, remember?" Jiovanni gave her a one-arm hug. "I'm proud of you, Zoe. What you did took guts. Aurora should be thanking you for saving Casa Di Moda instead of bad-mouthing you."

Her ears perked up, and she cranked her head in Jiovanni's direction. *Bad-mouthing me? What did Aurora say?* She opened her mouth to ask, but told herself it didn't matter. Zoe knew she'd done the right thing and was confident one day Aurora would realize it, too. In the meantime, she'd call in favors from her friends at various fashion magazines and work her connections. It was up to her to get the word out about the Chic and Curvy line, and she would. One post at a time. Going forward, the brand would be front and center on the social media pages. For her sake and for Casa Di Moda—she hoped the line was a smashing success.

"I know Aurora's your shero, and you think she's the best thing since platform sneakers were invented, but she has a history of using people, so be smart. Don't let her diminutive stature fool you. She's a she-devil in couture!"

"Then why are you working for her?"

His face paled, and his lips curled into a sneer. "Soon, Designs by Jiovanni, will take the fashion world by storm, and the years I wasted at Casa Di Moda will be a distant memory."

Bothered by his comments, Zoe held her tongue. All week he'd been in a funk, but whenever she tried to talk to him about his negative attitude, he'd brushed her off. Their colleagues were tired of his endless bitching and complaining about management, too. Aurora could be stubborn at times, but she was also thoughtful and generous, and Zoe wanted to see the fashion house succeed. It was a challenging time for the company, but she wanted to be part of the solution, not the problem.

"I told you this was a bad idea," Jiovanni grumbled. "We should go somewhere else."

The line wasn't moving, and the café was packed with wall-to-wall customers, but Zoe wasn't going anywhere until she had something to eat from her favorite café.

"You're shivering." Leaning over, Jiovanni wrapped her up in his arms and rubbed her shoulders. "Go inside and grab us a table."

"But you don't know what I want to order."

"Of course I do. You want an iced caramel latte with three sugars, two scoops of pistachio gelato, and one scoop of hazelnut gelato."

Beaming, Zoe rested a hand on her chest. "A man after my own heart."

"And don't you forget it."

Twenty minutes later, Jiovanni sat down at the corner table Zoe had found beside the window. Carrying a tray of food, he complained in Italian about the clerk who'd screwed up his order. To appease him, Zoe opened her neon-pink backpack, took out enough money to cover the entire bill and stuffed it into his shirt pocket. "Thanks, Jiovanni. It's on me."

"Great, now I have enough money to wine and dine Alessandra."

"That's the woman you met at the jazz bar, right? How are things going with her?"

"Wonderful. She's going to help me raise money to launch my fashion label."

"How? I thought she was a hotel manager at a fancy downtown hotel."

"She is, and she promised to provide me with intimate details about the rich."

"I'm confused." Zoe furrowed her brow. "Why do you need to know the whereabouts of hotel guests? How is that going to help you raise money for your fashion label?"

Jiovanni raised his cell in the air. "I'm now a paparazzo," he announced. "I'm going to take compromising photographs of celebrities. If they don't agree to buy them back from me, I'll sell them to the tabloids. I call it a win-win business deal."

"No, Jiovanni, it's called blackmail."

Zoe was so disappointed in him she didn't want to hear any more about his get-rich scheme. But she felt compelled to tell Jiovanni he was playing with fire. She warned him about the dangers of blackmailing rich people. Instead of addressing her concerns, he changed the subject. Blindsided by his question about Romeo, she stared down at her cup of gelato.

"Aurora said you and Romeo hit it off last night," he said, raising his coffee mug to his lips. "Is that true, or wishful thinking on her part?"

Heat warmed her skin. *We did more than just hit it off*, Zoe thought. *We kissed, and it was the most amazing ninety seconds of my life!*

The truth must have shown on her face, because his shoulders drooped. He made a noise in his throat, then coughed like a smoker on his deathbed.

"The media doesn't call Romeo the Sexy Devil for nothing."

Zoe wasn't one to kiss and tell, but she was excited about Romeo and wanted to tell Jiovanni about their incredible night. Before she could, he spoke in a somber tone of voice.

"Stay away from him," Jiovanni warned. "He's trouble with a capital T."

"You sound like Shelby. We talked this morning. She said I should play hard to get and make Romeo jump through hoops if he wants to be with me, but that's not me. I like him a lot, and I want to get to know him better, so that's what I'm going to do."

"Why would you want Romeo Morretti when you have me?"

"That's just nasty," she joked. "We could never date. You're like a brother to me—"

"Quit saying that," he snapped, raising his voice. "We're not family."

"We might as well be. You're a true friend, Jiovanni. I value your opinion, but you're wrong about Romeo. He's not the selfish womanizer the tabloids make him out to be."

"Yes, he is. He has a checkered past and a horrible track record with women. Don't believe me? Google him—you'll see that I'm right."

"Thanks for your concern, J, but I'm a smart cookie. I know what I'm doing."

"Do you? No disrespect, Zoe, but you're an easy target. I'm worried you'll get hurt."

An easy target? What is that supposed to mean?

"By your own admission, you've only had one serious relationship, so you have no idea how men operate. They can be ruthless, especially guys like Romeo Morretti."

"Don't worry about me. I can handle him."

And by handle, *you mean kiss him until you're breathless, right?* asked her inner voice.

"Fine, suit yourself, but don't come crying to me when he breaks your heart."

Worried she was going to lose her temper, Zoe admired the Christmas decorations inside the café. Giant paper ornaments hung from the ceiling, chairs were tied with red ribbons, and snowflakes were stuck to the window. Spotting a black sports car—that looked like something out of a James Bond movie—pull up to the curb, she noticed everyone on the street stop what they were doing to stare at the new arrival.

Jiovanni whistled. "Wow, what a beauty."

"You've seen one overpriced luxury car, you've seen them all."

"Did you know that the Alfa Romeo Disco Volante is one of the most coveted Italian sports cars in the world?" he asked, an awestruck expression on his face. "They only make a handful of them a year, and only the richest of the rich can afford the million-dollar price tag."

"What a waste of money. It's just a car—"

Jiovanni pressed a finger to her lips, and a giggle fell from Zoe's mouth.

"Woman, hush your mouth. It's not just a car. It's a work of art. Show some respect."

They laughed, and the tension hovering about their table disappeared.

The driver's-side door opened, and a dark-haired man in aviator sunglasses emerged. Zoe did a double take. Then another. *Romeo!* Goose bumps rippled across her skin as she watched her dreamy, brown-eyed crush march around the hood of the car. Opening the other door, Romeo helped his passenger to her feet and draped an arm around her shoulder. Zoe's stomach clenched. Surely her eyes were deceiving her. Blinking rapidly, Zoe struggled to focus her gaze.

Zoe leaned forward in her seat, couldn't take her eyes off Romeo and his date. With their creamy olive skin, dark hair and model-perfect features, they made a striking couple. As they headed toward the café, the crowd parted like the Red Sea. The brunette was fashionably dressed in a white fringe sweater, skinny jeans and beige heels, and Zoe suspected she was in the entertainment business. Watching them, she realized Romeo had lied to her about being single. Zoe wanted to run outside and confront him, but she forced herself to remain in her seat.

"I told you, Romeo Morretti isn't worth your time," Jiovanni said, a sympathetic expression on his face. "Do you want to leave?"

Picking up her spoon, she resumed eating her gelato. "No. Of course not."

"Just ignore him. Pretend he's not here."

Zoe scoffed. Romeo wasn't the kind of man a woman could ignore, but she was determined to try. Wanting to be a good friend, she turned away from the window, listening as Jiovanni chatted about his plans for New Year's Eve. Out of the corner of her eye, she saw the owner of the café sprint through the open door and greet Romeo and his date. Leading the couple inside the shop, he ushered them to the front of the line and filled their orders.

"Entitled bastard," Jiovanni grumbled. "Romeo gets preferential treatment everywhere he goes in Milan, and it's unfair. He's no better than anyone else. He should have to wait in line like the rest of us."

"Oh, stop, you use your looks to get preferential treatment all the time—"

The sound of Romeo's voice filled the air, and Zoe trailed off speaking.

"I was just talking about you, and here you are. *Che meravigliosa coincidenza.*"

Zoe froze. Her eyes were wide, her spoon was suspended in midair, and the walls of her throat were so thick she couldn't swallow. *What a wonderful coincidence? You're happy to see me? Really?* she thought, feeling as if she were having an out-of-body experience. "Romeo, what are you doing here?" she asked. "I thought you had to work today."

"I do, but Francesca dropped by the office and insisted I take her out for lunch," he explained. "She's my favorite sister, so of course I agreed."

Relief flooded Zoe's body. "That's so sweet of you, Romeo."

"Boy, please," Francesca said, swatting her brother's shoulder. "You're not fooling anyone with that good-boy act. I'm your *only* sister."

The siblings laughed, and watching them together made Zoe miss her sister.

Introductions were made, and everyone shook hands.

"So, *you're* Zoe," Francesca said, cocking an eyebrow. "Very interesting."

For the second time in minutes, Zoe didn't know what to say or think.

"Romeo's been talking my ear off about you ever since we left his office, and now that we've met, I can see why. You're stunning." Francesca flicked a finger in the air. "I love your outfit. Is it from Casa Di Moda?"

Zoe touched her chest. *You do?* Her long-sleeved plaid jumper was a gift from Jiovanni, and she loved how it fit her shape. "Yes, as a matter of fact it is. Jiovanni designed it," she said, proudly. "In fact, he's been dressing me ever since I arrived in Milan."

"I was stoked to hear about Casa Di Moda's plus-size line. How exciting!"

"Jiovanni is the creative force behind the line, and with him at the helm, it's going to be a runaway hit. He's talented and creative, and all of his designs are outstanding."

The owner appeared, carrying a tray filled with food, and put it down on the table.

"We'd love to hear more about the line," Romeo asked. "Can we join you?"

Zoe started to speak, but Jiovanni interrupted her.

"No, sorry, we were just leaving. Enjoy your lunch. Ciao!"

Zoe gave her best friend a funny look. He never missed an opportunity to flirt with an attractive woman or boast about his fresh, cutting-edge designs. She was surprised when he grabbed her hand and dragged her out of the ice cream shop. "What was that all about?" she asked, perplexed by his odd behavior. "You love meeting new people. Why didn't you want to hang out with Romeo and his sister?"

"Today you're mine, all mine, and I don't want the Morretti family interrupting our fun."

He draped an arm around her shoulder and gave her a wet, sloppy kiss on the cheek.

"You're crazy!" she said with a laugh.

They crossed the intersection arm in arm. Out of the corner of her eye, Zoe noticed Romeo watching them from the café window and hoped she hadn't blown her chance with the drop-dead gorgeous tycoon with the killer smile.

Chapter 13

"I think we should sever ties with Capone Costruzioni," Simona announced, clasping her hands together on the conference room table at Morretti Finance and Investments on Wednesday morning. "Mr. Capone blames the economic crisis for his company's financial woes, but his poor management and organization skills are to blame. Worse still, he treats people like crap."

Seated at the head of the mahogany table, reviewing the stack of business contracts his attorney had dropped off minutes earlier, Romeo listened as his chief operating officer complained about the owner of the beleaguered construction company. Morretti Finance and Investments had hundreds of clients around the world, and Romeo took great pride in connecting with his investors on a regular basis. There was nothing his employees could tell him that he didn't already know, but he enjoyed Simona's weekly updates and nodded his head as she spoke. He'd never met a more tenacious woman, and Romeo was thankful the Princeton graduate was an integral part of his executive team.

"All business isn't good business, and I think Mr. Capone is a liability. I'm worried he's going to do something to embarrass us, so it's imperative we act now…"

Tapping his diamond ink pen on his file folder, Romeo considered Simona's words. His gaze strayed to the wall clock hanging above the door, and he wondered what his favorite PR director was up to. Since running into Zoe at the gelato shop ten days ago, he'd seen her every night of the week. Without fail, he'd drop by Casa Di Moda at the end of her workday and convince her to have dinner with him. They'd talk and flirt for hours at a nearby pub. Romeo could always count on Zoe to make him laugh. Some nights they'd have dinner at a quaint, out-of-the-way bistro; other nights they'd check out a jazz bar or watch Christmas movies at her cozy studio apartment. Three weeks after meeting her, Romeo was ready to take himself off the market. "No ring, no rules," used to be his dating motto, but he didn't want Zoe unless he could have all of her—her heart, her mind and her body—and he didn't want to share her with anyone else. She was special to him, someone he could be himself around. There was nothing fake or pretentious about her. Zoe lived her life in an authentic way, and that appealed to him— "I know you rarely drop clients, but I hope you'll consider what I've said."

The sound of Simona's voice yanked Romeo out of his thoughts. "I take it your meeting last night with Mr. Capone at El Porteno didn't go well."

Her cheeks turned as red as an apple. Simona wore a troubled expression on her face, and Romeo felt guilty for not giving his COO his undivided attention. What had Zoe said yesterday? *You're a workaholic who's obsessed with*

making money, and you need to change your ways. Then
she'd plucked his cell phone out of his hands, dropped it
into her snakeskin purse and dragged him out onto the
dance floor at the Hollywood nightclub. Was it true? Had
he fallen back into his old habits? And most importantly,
was he putting his health at risk?

Romeo considered his furious work schedule. He did
his best thinking on the treadmill, so he woke up every
morning at the crack of dawn to jog eight miles. Exercis-
ing helped to clear his head, and three times a week he also
took a tae kwon do class with his executive team. Building strong relationships with his employees was the key
to his success, and he enjoyed getting to know his staff
better. Romeo never forgot what it was like being a lowly
associate at a successful financial institute in Milan, so
he made a point to touch base with everyone who worked
at Morretti Finance and Investments regularly.

Simona's cell phone pinged, and she picked it up off
the table. "Oh, no, I just got an email from Mr. Capone.
He's threatening to…to…" She trailed off. She dropped
her cell on the table and glared at the device as if it were
her mortal enemy.

"He's threatening to do what? Talk to me, Simona. I
want to help." Last year, when he'd been away on three
months' medical leave, she'd done an outstanding job running the office in his absence. Romeo wanted to support
her now. "What happened last night?"

Simona picked up her mug and sipped her coffee.

"Should I call Mr. Capone and ask him, or are you
going to tell me?"

"It was nothing. He had too much to drink and crossed
the line, but I handled it."

Setting aside his contracts, Romeo took off his reading
glasses and stared at his COO. Slender with curly black

hair, the Venice native looked more like a preschool teacher than a brilliant investment banker with decades of experience. "He made a pass at you during your meeting and you shot him down, didn't you?"

"No," she said, a smirk twisting her peach lips. "He grabbed my ass in the parking lot. I slapped him so hard his glasses flew off his face and landed in a mud puddle!"

Romeo cracked up. Picturing the scene in his mind's eye—his soft-spoken COO, slapping the crap out of the burly construction worker—made him chuckle so hard his body shook. "Damn, Simona. That's the funniest thing I've heard in a long time," he said, shaking his head in disbelief. "Thanks for the laugh."

Her eyes widened. "You're not mad at me for losing my cool?"

"Why would I be mad at you? You handled the situation perfectly."

"Mr. Capone says he has a black eye. He's threatening to file a police report."

Romeo scoffed. "I'd like to see him try. Ignore him. He's bluffing."

"What about his contract? Do we have to honor it?"

"Not if he put his hands on you. I'm behind you one hundred percent, Simona, so prepare the necessary paperwork and have the legal team review it."

Simona sighed. "Great. I'll get right on it and follow up with you at Blue Bar tonight."

"I have plans, so let's touch base tomorrow morning."

"You're skipping out on drinks with the executive team again? How come? You used to encourage everyone to go, and lately you're a no-show."

Romeo wanted to tell Simona about Zoe, but thought better of it and shrugged. Thirsty, he reached for his mug. Realizing it was empty, he decided to go to the staff

room for more. He'd been in the conference room from
for hours—returning phone calls, proofreading contracts,
rewriting mistake-ridden proposals—and he wanted to
stretch his legs before the eleven o'clock board meeting.
"Let's go make some fresh coffee," he proposed as he stood
up and opened the door. "It's going to be a long day, and
we're going to need some caffeine."

"Speak for yourself. I did yoga this morning and I feel
great. *You* should try it sometime."

Laughing, they exited the conference room and walked
down the corridor. The scents of peppermint and cinnamon
overwhelmed his senses. To please Simona and the rest of
his Christmas-loving staff, he'd agreed to let them decorate
the office, but they'd gone overboard. Strings of miniature
lights lined the windowsill, velvet stockings were displayed
on the walls, and candy canes, colored ornaments and gingerbread men hung from the Santa-themed tree. It had a belt
and a red tutu. Every time Romeo looked at it he chuckled.

The office was quiet except for the sound of the ringing
telephones, but Romeo knew his staff was hard at work. He
spotted two men in dark suits enter the reception area and
suspected they were cops. The man in the sunglasses had
a gruff demeanor, and his partner wore a terse expression
on his fleshy face. Romeo's gut was telling him something
was wrong, so instead of ducking into the staff room to
feed his caffeine addiction, he stalked into the waiting area.

"Good morning, Officers."

Romeo put his empty coffee mug on the glass desk
and slid his hands into the pockets of his gray pin-striped
suit. It was a gift from Davide, but every time he wore it
he thought about Zoe. She meant a lot to him. He was so
excited about their relationship, he wanted to spend all of
his free time with her. He'd cleared his schedule for the

weekend so they could hang out at his villa, but he still had to convince her to be his guest.

"I'm Romeo Morretti, and this is my chief operating officer, Simona Vitti," he explained, nodding his head in greeting. "What can we do for you today?"

Double Chin flashed his badge, then introduced his short balding partner with the chipped front tooth. "We have a sensitive matter to discuss with you," he said in a quiet tone of voice. "Is there somewhere we can speak in private?"

"Yes, of course, right this way, Officers. We can talk in my office."

Leading the group through the corridor, Romeo tried to figure out why the police were at his company. His thoughts ran wild, jumping from one theory to the next. Maybe they wanted to discuss his speeding tickets. But why would they waste their time? It was only a few thousand euros, and the late penalty was minimal. Besides, he'd racked up speeding tickets numerous times before and never received a visit from Milan's finest.

Entering his office, Romeo was temporary blinded by the intensity of the sun and closed the window blinds. He offered the detectives something to drink from the bar, but they declined and sat down in the padded armchairs in front of his desk.

"To what do we owe this pleasure?" he asked, anxious to get down to business. He had an executive board meeting in forty-five minutes and wanted the officers long gone before it started. "Is this about my speeding tickets? If it is, I can pay them today."

Double Chin reached into his suit jacket, took out a photograph and dropped it on the desk. Romeo picked it up and a cold chill flooded his body.

"Do you know who the man in that mug shot is?"

Simona took the picture from Romeo's hand and

dropped it on the table. "Yes, of course. It's Julio Mario Domínguez. I signed him to Morretti Investments last year, and we have a great business relationship. In fact, he's one of our most successful investors."

"Were you aware of his ties to organized crime when you took him on as a client?"

Romeo was taken aback by the question, but he wore a blank expression on his face. "Every investment we've done on his behalf in the past year has been legal, by the book."

Chipped Tooth snarled like a pit bull. "You knew full well about his shady business practices and criminal endeavors. *You* handled his money."

It was a statement, not a question, but Romeo wasn't afraid to set him straight. "As with most of our clients, we only handled a small fraction of his income. Fifteen percent to be exact."

"Fifteen percent of a billion dollars is a substantial amount of money, Mr. Morretti."

Double Chin leveled a finger at him. "That's chump change to a man like you, but regular folks like me think a hundred and fifty million euros is a ton of money. If we find out you're lying we'll prosecute you and everyone at this company to the full extent of the law."

"Do you have proof that a crime has been committed?" Simona asked, pursing her lips.

"Julio Mario Domínguez was arrested in Paris this morning and charged with money laundering for a notorious Colombian drug dealer with a lengthy criminal record."

Romeo glanced at Simona. She didn't even bat an eyelash. Detectives had revealed pertinent information about the criminal case against Julio Mario Domínguez, but his COO maintained her calm disposition. As always, he could count on her to have his back.

"With all due respect, Detectives, I don't understand

why you're here," Romeo said, projecting confidence, even though sweat was dribbling down the back of his dress shirt. "If Mr. Domínguez was arrested, then there must be a strong case against him. Why are you here, interrupting our busy workday?"

Leaning forward in his seat, Double Chin wore a twisted smile on his mouth. "Because Julio Mario Domínguez named *you* as his co-conspirator."

The hair on the back of his neck shot up, but Romeo remained perfectly still.

"My guess? Domínguez is probably cutting a deal with French authorities as we speak."

"That's ludicrous," Simona said. "He's lying to save his neck."

"I don't think so. I think Mr. Domínguez has a very compelling story."

Simona pointed a finger at her chest. "I'm the one who handled Mr. Domínguez's personal investments, not Romeo. Furthermore, neither one of us has anything to hide."

"The way I see it, you have two choices. Cooperate with authorities or face jail time."

Chipped Tooth glanced around the office. "We need to see your financial records."

"And I'll need to see a warrant."

The detectives shared a look, and Romeo knew they didn't have one. Thanks to Markos, he knew his legal rights, and once Tweedledee and Tweedledum left his office, he would be calling his brother. His family was coming to Milan for the Christmas Wonderland Ball, but this was an emergency, and Romeo needed to speak to Markos as soon as possible. Before he was arrested for a crime he didn't commit.

"You have seventy-two hours to decide."

"But we're swamped with work right now," Simona argued. "Surely this can wait until the New Year."

"Justice waits for no man." Chipped Tooth stood and buttoned his wrinkled gray suit. "It would be in your best interest not to repeat the details of this conversation with anyone. It could compromise the investigation. I'd hate to see you charged with obstruction of justice."

Stretching, as if he'd just taken a power nap, Double Chin rose from his chair.

"We'll be back," Chipped Tooth said, with a curt nod.

"Don't forget your warrant next time."

Simona offered to walk the detectives out, and Romeo was so glad to see them leave his office he sighed in relief. He needed a moment to catch his breath. To think things through. To regain control before he called Markos.

The detectives' threats loomed in his mind. Was it true? Had one of his richest clients been arrested for money laundering? Did Mr. Domínguez have ties to criminal organizations, or had the police made a grave mistake?

Taking his cell out of his pocket, Romeo accessed the internet. Every morning, he read the local newspapers and his favorite business magazines, but there'd been no mention of Julio Mario Domínguez being arrested in Paris. Still, his heart raced.

How could this happen? Every month, he contacted his clients to ensure they had no major issues and concerns… Romeo bolted upright in his chair. Is that why the Colombian businessman had been dodging his calls? Because he was busy cutting deals with the authorities? He shuddered to think what would happen if the story got out. If his esteemed clients discovered he'd been accused of money laundering.

Romeo gulped. It would destroy him, cripple his financial empire and ruin his reputation. To clear his head, he stood and moved to the window. Staring out at the bright blue sky, he feared his first Christmas with Zoe was going to be memorable for all the wrong reasons.

Chapter 14

"Wrong, wrong, wrong," Zoe complained, pitching clothes over her shoulder and onto the bedroom floor. Standing in front of her closet on Friday night searching for an outfit to wear to the Il Divo concert—when Romeo was due at her apartment in an hour—was stressful, but Zoe was determined to find the perfect dress for their five o'clock date. It was a miracle she'd made it home from work on time. All afternoon she'd been promoting the Christmas holiday line and the Men of Milan calendar. If she didn't have plans with Romeo, she'd still be at the office tweeting and blogging on Casa Di Moda's social media pages.

Heat flushed her cheeks, warming her body all over. Just the thought of seeing Romeo again made her pulse race. What a difference a few weeks make, Zoe thought, as treasured memories filled her heart. Last night, after the Christmas tree lighting ceremony, they'd strolled the streets hand in hand. Romeo had been quiet and with-drawn, seemed to be in another world. It was obvious his mind was still at work, but when she'd asked him what was wrong, he'd apologized for ignoring her and kissed her passionately on the lips.

Surprised by Romeo's public display of affection, she'd pressed herself flat against him and wrapped her arms around his waist. Days earlier, while they were cooking dinner together in the gourmet kitchen at his penthouse, they'd agreed to keep their relationship quiet. Every day, her colleagues grilled her about her love life, but she skill-fully evaded their questions. She knew Jiovanni was upset with her for not confiding in him, but Zoe wanted to honor Romeo's request. After everything his ex-fiancée had put him through, he was leery about dating in the public eye, and Zoe didn't blame him.

Reflecting on their marathon date, Zoe couldn't recall ever having so much fun. The area was a popular hangout spot among millennials, and they'd spent the evening sam-pling popular Christmas desserts, mulled wine and roasted chestnuts. The Navigli district was known for its canals, and when Romeo suggested a boat ride, she'd agreed. Zoe would remember their trip to Lake Maggiore as long as she lived. Nestled in Romeo's arms, staring at the star-filled sky, she'd felt as if she were in another era. Zoe didn't know how it happened, but one minute they were snapping selfies together and the next Romeo was kiss-ing her passionately. When Romeo drove her home at the end of the night, she invited him inside for a cup of cof-fee, and they'd wasted no time picking up where they'd left off on the boat.

Zoe ran her hands along the bodice of the snug-fitting, deep red gown she'd found in the back of her closet, then yanked it off the velvet hanger. *If this doesn't knock Ro-*

meo's socks off, I don't know what will! she thought, laughing to herself.

Chucking her satin bathrobe on the canopy bed, Zoe slipped on the dress and scrutinized her appearance. Feeling chic and sophisticated in the gown Jiovanni had made for her months earlier, she admired her profile in the floor-length mirror. The capped sleeves and cinched waist flattered her hourglass figure, but she worried about tripping on the long ruffled train. Romeo made her nervous, on edge, and when he touched her anything could happen.

Zoe wet her lips with her tongue. Last night in her living room, one sensuous kiss had led to another, and in the blink of an eye they were moaning and groaning, desperately pawing at each other's clothes. Overcome with need, they'd made out on the couch for hours.

Her cell phone rang. Remembering the last place she'd seen it, she raced inside the bathroom and scooped it off the counter. Zoe read the name and number on the screen. It was her mom calling from New York. Even though she had a date to get ready for, she wanted to check in with her family. Wanting to "see" her mother, she pressed the Video button and laughed as her mom waved and blew kisses.

"Hi, baby girl. How are you doing?"

"Great. I'm just getting ready to go out for dinner."

"With Jiovanni? Again? You spend *way* too much time with that boy."

Laughing, Zoe picked up her favorite bottle of perfume off the counter and sprayed her neck and wrist. "Mom, I've told you a million times, we're just friends."

"Good, I don't want Khalil to think he has any competition."

Zoe was annoyed with her mom, but she spoke in a calm voice, didn't let her frustration show. "Mom, you have to move on. Khalil and I are not getting back together—"

"He's still crazy about you, you know."

"Mom, we haven't spoken to each other in months," she pointed out.

"Together forever, never apart. Sometimes in distance, but never in heart."

Zoe hated when her mother quoted inspirational sayings and wished her dad were around to help her talk some sense into her. Noticing the time on her cell phone, she propped it against the tissue box so she could finish getting ready for her date.

"When will you be home? Have you booked your flight? Are you staying for a month?"

Her body tensed. All week, she'd been dreading this moment. The last thing Zoe wanted to do was disappoint her parents, and she knew they'd be crushed when she told them the bad news, but she couldn't keep putting it off. "Mom, I won't be coming home for the holidays."

The smile slid off her face. "Why not? Didn't you get your Christmas bonus?"

"No, and my credit cards are all maxed out," she explained. "I just can't afford it."

"I'm not surprised. Milan is one of the most expensive cities in the world. Even though your dad and I told you it was a bad idea, you just had to take a job there."

Her dad peered over her mom's shoulder, wearing a broad grin, and Zoe smiled. Her parents couldn't be more different. Statuesque with burgundy locks, Collette Smith loved to socialize and make new friends. Not her husband of thirty-five years, whom she'd met in grade school in Trinidad. Slender with dark brown skin, Reuben Smith was a soft-spoken man who'd rather watch CNN than party. But their personalities complemented each other perfectly.

"Zoe, is that you, baby girl?" he asked. "How is life treating you in Milan?"

Before Zoe could respond to her dad's question, her mom spoke up.

"It's terrible. Our daughter can't come home for Christmas because she's flat broke."

"Baby girl, don't worry," Reuben said in a soothing voice. "I'll buy your ticket."

"Dad, don't. I have to work. There's no way I'll get the time off this late in the game."

Her mom snapped her fingers. "Fine, then we'll come see you."

"Good idea, honey. We're retired. Why not go see our hardworking daughter in Milan for a few weeks? Shelby is thinking of volunteering in Peru again this Christmas, so we might as well visit you, Zoe." Reuben nodded so hard his eyeglasses slid down his thin nose. "I'll call the travel agent first thing tomorrow to see what flights are available."

Zoe missed her parents, but she didn't want them flying to Milan during the holidays. The plane tickets would be ridiculously expensive; the airports would be a jam-packed. Zoe didn't want her parents flying during the busiest time of the year. "No. Don't. I'll be home in February," she explained, speaking in a cheery voice, though her heart was sad. "We can hang out then."

"Christmas won't be the same without you."

The doorbell rang, and Zoe groaned. "Oh, no, Romeo's early, and I'm not ready!"

"Who's Romeo?" Reuben asked, furrowing his brow. "Is he one of your colleagues?"

No, Dad, he's the guy I've fallen hard for, Zoe thought, but didn't dare say. She had strong feelings for Romeo and wanted to tell her parents about him, but it was too soon. They'd only been seeing each other for a few weeks; there was no guarantee their red-hot relationship would last. "Mom, Dad, I have to go, but I'll call you on the weekend."

"Be safe, honey, and remember what I said about Jiovanni. He seems like a nice guy, but he's not the right man for you so don't let him charm you."

Zoe laughed. "Okay, Mom, I won't, and you remember what I said about Khalil."

"Don't be silly. Of course you're going to get back together. You're soul mates."

The doorbell rang again, but Zoe couldn't end the call until she set her mother straight.

"Mom, Khalil and I are over. He's moved on with his life, and so have I."

Her dad nodded his head in understanding, and Zoe was grateful for his support.

"Baby girl, as long as you're happy we're happy."

"Like hell we are!" her mom said, puckering her thin lips. "Khalil's practically family, and his mother and I have been dear friends for many years. You *have* to marry him."

"No, I don't, Mom. It's my choice, not yours."

"You've been in Milan for two years, but you still haven't met anyone who lights your fire." Collette wore a triumphant smile. "Face it. No one will ever be able to measure up to Khalil. He's your first love and your only love. No one can take his place in your heart."

"I'm crazy about Romeo, and I want to have a future with him."

Zoe cupped a hand over her mouth. She couldn't believe she'd revealed her innermost thoughts and wished she could stuff the words back down her throat.

"Y-Y-You're what?" Collette stammered. "Where did you meet this guy? Who is he? What does he do for a living?"

Her cell phone buzzed, cueing her that she had an incoming call, but Zoe didn't answer it.

"Romeo is a successful businessman with real estate properties all over the world," Zoe boasted. She tried to temper her excitement, but it seeped into her tone. "We haven't know each other long, but he's a good man, and I enjoy his company."

"That's wonderful, baby girl. We look forward to meeting him in the near future."

Collette scoffed. "Speak for yourself. Khalil will always be my first and *only* choice."

Zoe almost rolled her eyes, but since she didn't want to do anything to set her mother off again, she said goodbye to her parents. "Bye, Mom. Bye, Dad. I love you."

"We love you, too. Have fun tonight, and give Romeo Morretti my regards," her dad said cheerfully.

"You know who he is?" she asked, raising an eyebrow. "How?"

"I just Googled him. His cousin Demetri is one of the greatest baseball players of all time, so be a good daughter and get an autograph for your old man. I'm a huge fan."

"I'll see what I can do."

Her dad pumped his fist in the air. "That's my girl!"

Shocked to see the time on her cell, Zoe ended the call and exited the bathroom. She hoped Romeo wasn't mad at her for making him wait outside, and sent him a text message explaining why she was running behind schedule.

"There you are, bellissima. How are your parents?"

Zoe stopped. Glancing up from her cell, her eyes widened. Confused, she couldn't make sense of what was going on. *What is Romeo doing in my living room? How did he get in? The doors locked!*

"I rang the buzzer several times, but you didn't answer," he explained, sliding his hands into the pockets of his slacks. "I tried the door and it opened, so I decided to wait for you in here. I hope that's okay."

Thinking back to the afternoon, Zoe slowly nodded her head. "I got home late from work, and I was in such a rush to get ready, I must have forgotten to lock it when I came in."

"You have to be more careful. A stranger could waltz right in and catch you off guard."

"Don't worry about me. I kickbox, and I'm not afraid to use it."

"Thanks for the heads-up. I'll have to remember not to piss you off."

He reached for her hand, and her heart swooned. It happened every time Romeo touched her. He'd mastered the art of looking suave and sophisticated, and being in his presence did a number on her libido. Short of breath, her erect nipples strained against her lace push-up bra, dying for release. It took supreme effort, but Zoe tore her eyes away from his mouth and forced herself to quit fantasizing about ripping the clothes off his muscled body.

Romeo whistled. "Wow, Zoe, you're sensational."

"You say that every time you see me."

"That's because it's true. You never cease to amaze me. I love your elegant style."

"Thanks, Romeo. You look great, too." Admiring how handsome he was in his blue collared dress shirt and black pants.

"I'm almost ready. Just give me five minutes to do my makeup, and I'll be good to go."

"You don't need any. You're perfect just the way you are." Stepping forward, he captured her around the waist and held her close to his chest. "You're stunning, Zoe, and I'm in awe of your natural beauty."

"Then imagine how much better I'd look with mascara and lipstick."

"It's impossible to improve perfection," he whispered,

brushing his lips against the curve of her ear. "Did you pack an overnight bag like I asked?"

Pulling out of his arms, she stared up at him in disbelief. "Was I supposed to?"

"Last night during the boat ride, I told you I wanted to spend the weekend with you."

"I thought you were joking."

Romeo gestured to the bedroom door. "I wasn't. So go grab your stuff. I'll wait."

Zoe hesitated; she didn't know how to put her feelings into words without offending him and took a moment to process her thoughts. She loved the idea of hanging out with Romeo at his countryside villa for a few days, but she didn't want to give him the wrong idea. His past was a huge obstacle for her to overcome, and there were times she couldn't help feeling that she was fighting a losing battle. "I don't know if I'm ready for a sexual relationship."

"I understand. I'm okay with that," he said, tenderly rubbing her shoulders.

Zoe wondered if the word *sucker* was stamped on her forehead and shot him a you're-not-fooling-me look. "Really? You don't mind waiting a month? Or three? Or even six?"

"No. I don't, and furthermore I'd never pressure you to have sex. Contrary to what the media thinks, I'm not that kind of guy. It'll happen when we're both ready, and I'm prepared to wait as long as it takes."

Moved by his honesty, Zoe couldn't stop a smile from curling the corners of her mouth.

"You're special to me, and I don't want to lose you."

"Seriously? You're not just saying that to impress me?"

"I don't have to lie to impress you. I have adoring fans all over the city, remember?"

Romeo wiggled his eyebrows and Zoe cracked up, laughing long and hard.

"Okay, I'll come, but don't get any funny ideas. We're *not* knockin' boots this weekend."

A mischievous expression covered his face. "Why not? That's my favorite song!"

"Of course it is. You're the quintessential ladies' man."

"Not anymore. I'm a one-woman man." Romeo kissed her lips. "I'm your man."

His confession blew her mind, and seconds passed before she regained her voice. "You're serious?"

"Absolutely. And now that we're a couple, you'll have to make more room in your schedule for me. Ideally, I'd like to see you every day, but I know how busy you are at work, so I'm willing to compromise. Six dates a week sounds reasonable to me, don't you think?"

He tightened his hold around her waist and spoke in a silky, smooth voice.

"We have an incredible connection, and I'm excited to see what the future holds for us."

Her pulse was pounding out of control and it hurt to swallow, but Zoe pushed the question in her mind out of her dry mouth. "You want us to be exclusive? You're sure?"

"I'd love nothing more." Romeo brushed his nose against hers. "I have feelings for you, Zoe, and I don't want to compete with anyone else for your time and affection. It's time to change the status on your social media pages from 'single' to 'in a relationship.'"

Dumbstruck, Zoe couldn't believe what she was hearing. Was shocked by Romeo's candor, his openness.

"And one more thing," he continued, kissing the corners of her lips. "Tell Jiovanni and the other guys you work with who have the hots for you, you're spoken for..."

Romeo was way off base, dead wrong about her colleagues, but she didn't argue with him. Couldn't when he was playing in her hair and stroking her arms and hips. Zoe liked what he was doing with his hands, enjoyed feeling them against her flesh. No one had ever spoken to her in that tone before, and his bold attitude was a turn-on. Made her wet. They'd only known each other for a few weeks, but it felt like months had passed since their fateful meeting in November, and Zoe was moved—and aroused—by his words.

"I'll be back in a minute," she said, giving Romeo a peck on the lips. "Wait right here."

Feeling on top of the world, Zoe hurried down the hall and into her bedroom at the rear of the apartment. After putting on mascara and some red lipstick, she tossed toiletries, clothes and her journal into her overnight bag and zipped it up.

Zoe put on her stilettos and adjusted her dress. Catching sight of Romeo in her peripheral vision, she only hoped that when they arrived at his villa at the end of the night, her hormones wouldn't get her into any trouble. She desired him more than she'd ever wanted anyone, and liked the idea of breaking the rules with her dreamy crush.

Chapter 15

La Piastra Calda was known for its innovative cuisine, exceptional service and swank decor. Zoe knew from reading local newspapers that it routinely hosted diplomats, heads of state and British royalty. Like many of the best restaurants in the country, La Piastra Calda was family-owned with a devoted clientele and a six-month waiting list for reservations.

"I hope you brought your appetite, because I heard the dishes at La Piastra Calda are out of this world." Romeo helped Zoe out of the passenger seat of his Spada Vetture Sport and draped an arm around her waist. "I've never been here before, but if the food's even half as good as my brother Enrique says it is, then it's going to be a very delicious night."

The valet opened the front door and stepped aside to let them pass. *"Godere!"*

Zoe couldn't believe her eyes. The employees were

standing at attention in the waiting area and bowed in greeting as they entered the restaurant. Embarrassed that everyone in the room was staring at them, Zoe pretended to admire the colorful string art hanging on the walls.

A man with a bushy mustache stepped forward and introduced himself. "Welcome to La Piastra, Mr. Morretti," he bellowed. "I'm the owner and head chef of this fine establishment. It's an honor to have you here with us. If there is anything we can do to enhance your dining experience, please don't hesitate to ask."

The owner clasped his hands together, then gestured to the spiral staircase. "If you'll follow me, I'll show you to your private second-floor table."

Hearing noise and laughter coming from inside the restaurant, Zoe peered over the owner's shoulder and scanned the room. Saturated with ivory and various shades of blue, the dining area and adjoining lounge were packed with well-dressed diners. Zoe couldn't help gawking at the famous faces eating just an arm's length away from her.

The second floor was decked out in stone and glass. The elaborate chandeliers hanging from the vaulted ceiling beautified the space. The air smelled of pinecones and garland, and the refreshing scent reminded Zoe of how much fun she'd had in the summer with Jiovanni and their friends. They'd done it all: barbecued at neighborhood parks, fished and camped at Lake Garda, and danced at music festivals. Though Zoe couldn't imagine anything better than attending the Il Divo concert with Romeo later that evening.

"Since it's the holidays, I couldn't resist decorating the table in bright, festive colors," the owner said with a proud smile. "I trust that everything is to your liking…"

The round table in the middle the dining room had gleaming silverware, gold, silk linens and a bouquet filled with poinsettias. Hundreds of miniature candles twinkled, and the female pianist played "It's the Most Wonderful Time of Year" quietly in the background.

"This is one of our finest and most popular wines." Beaming, he picked up the gold-and-black bottle off the table, opened it, and filled their glasses to the brim. "Your server will be here shortly with your first course."

The owner nodded, then marched toward the staircase, his toothy smile still in place.

"That's odd," Zoe said, glancing around the room. "How come it's jam-packed downstairs, with dozens of people waiting for a table, but empty up here?"

Romeo pulled out her chair. "Because I rented out the second floor for our date. Every time we go out for dinner, you strike up a conversation with the people seated nearby, or end up making a new friend at the lounge or bar—"

"You have a problem with me being nice?" she said, taking a seat at the table. "Why?"

Romeo picked up his napkin, draped it across his legs and plucked a piece of toasted garlic bread out of the bread-basket. "No, of course not, but I'd like to spend a quiet evening with my girl without every Tom, Dick and Harry flirting with you. Is that too much to ask?"

Hearing Romeo call her his girl gave Zoe a rush, made her feel warm inside.

"Don't you think you're exaggerating a tad bit?" she asked, pinching two fingers together. "I'm a PR direc-tor, not a famous reality TV star with a billion Twitter followers."

"You might as well be. You attract attention wherever you go, and I'd be lying if I said I like it. I don't. The truth is, I want you all to myself tonight."

The waiter arrived with the first course, and while they ate their Tuscan chickpea soup, they discussed their busy workday, how talented the pianist was and the menu Romeo had created with the head chef for their date. "It has nine courses?" she repeated, bewildered by his words. "That's insane. I enjoy a good meal as much as the next girl, but I'll never be able to eat that much food. My waist-line won't forgive me if I do!"

"As the popular Italian saying goes, 'the appetite comes from eating.' I suspect as the night wears on you'll care less about the calories and more about the next delicious course."

Wanting to know more about the acclaimed restaurant, Zoe picked up the menu, opened it and read the short paragraph about its forty-year history. Impressed with the owner's bio, she flipped to the second page and scanned the list of dishes.

Her eyes widened. Five hundred euros per person? Two thousand euros for their bottle of wine? Twenty-five percent gratuity? Fanning her face with the menu, she swallowed hard. Zoe didn't want to even think about how much Romeo had shelled out to rent out the second floor of the five-star restaurant, but her curiosity got the best of her. Zoe asked Romeo for details, but he changed the subject. He questioned her about Casa Di Moda, and she forgot about the restaurant's outrageous prices and chatted excitedly about her job and her colleagues. "I feel fortunate to be at Casa Di Moda," Zoe said, speaking from her heart. "Every company has its issues, and some days are better than others, but I'm happy at the fashion house and I wouldn't want to work anywhere else."

"What are your long-term plans? How much longer do you plan to live in Milan?"

"I don't know." Zoe took a piece of garlic bread from the basket, and tasted it. It was warm and moist, and she was so hungry she quickly finished it. "I miss my family. It's hard being away from them, especially during the holidays, but I've always dreamed of living and working abroad. I'm not ready to leave Milan just yet."

The waiter arrived with the second course, placed everything on the table, then left.

Zoe picked up her fork and tasted the squid Bolognese, savored the unique flavors tickling her taste buds. The appetizer was packed with so many spices Zoe pressed her eyes shut and moaned in appreciation.

"If you met the right guy, would you consider living in Milan permanently?"

"I don't know. It's hard to say. Italy's a long way from home."

Romeo shook his head. "Not if you have a private jet at your disposal."

"You're *so* right. What was I thinking? I'll tell Aurora and Davide to have their Boeing 727 ready for Monday." Zoe snapped her fingers. "Oh shucks, I forgot they don't have one."

"I do. Anytime you want to use it, just ask. *Il mio getto è vostro jet.*"

Zoe raised an eyebrow. *My jet is your jet? He can't be serious!* Convinced he was teasing her, she picked up her glass and took a sip. The fruity liquid took the edge off her nerves, helped her to relax even though Romeo was gazing at her intently.

"What about you?" she asked, deciding it was his turn to be in the hot seat. "Have you always wanted to be an investment banker, or did your parents encourage your career path?"

"When I was a kid my dream was to become a professional tap dancer, just like my idol, Gregory Hines. But my father threatened to disown me if I didn't get my MBA, so I gave it up."

"You can tap-dance? No way! Are you any good?"

Nodding, he wiped his mouth with his napkin, then dropped it on his empty salad bowl. "Of course I was good. I studied tap for several years. My instructor said I had raw, natural talent. I wanted to move to the States to study at the University of the Arts in the City of Brotherly Love. It's one of the most prestigious dance schools in the world…"

"I don't believe you. You're pulling my leg."

Romeo stood. "Normally, I don't tap-dance to slow songs, but what the heck. There's a first time for everything, so here goes."

Intrigued, Zoe put down her fork and stared at him intently. *What is he doing?*

Tapping his feet in rhythm to the music, he lifted his leg high in the air and tapped the ball of his foot against the floor. Romeo rocked back and forth, bouncing from one leg to the next, swinging and shuffling his long limbs. He swung his arms in time to the beat, and watching him make music with his feet excited her. He moved with such ease and confidence, Zoe was mesmerized, couldn't take her eyes off him. The pianist finished playing "The Little Drummer Boy," and Romeo struck a pose—head cocked, arms crossed, eyebrows raised. Forgetting she was at an upscale restaurant and not a sporting event, Zoe surged to her feet, cheering at the top of her lungs. "Romeo, that was incredible!" she praised, blown away by his impromptu performance. "You come alive when you tap-dance. It's amazing to see."

Returning to the table, Romeo took his seat, grabbed his glass and took a sip of his ice water. "I haven't danced in years, but that was a lot of fun. It brought back good memories."

"How did you learn to dance like that?"

"Fred Astaire. My mom used to watch his movies when I was a kid, and to make her laugh, I'd try to imitate his moves." He wore a twisted smile. "My mom thought I had talent and enrolled me in dance classes. Everything was great until my dad found out."

Zoe leaned forward in her seat, eager to hear more.

"He told me I needed to be 'a man,' and that I'd never make it as a tap dancer, so I got my business degree at the University of Milan, and my MBA in international business a couple years later."

"Do you regret not pursuing your dream of being a tap dancer?"

His jaw clenched, but he spoke in a calm voice. "Life's too short for regrets."

"I know, I know, life's about closing deals, making money and wooing clients," she quipped, quoting him verbatim. "But do you wish you had done things differently? Do you regret not following in the footsteps of your childhood idol, Gregory Hines?"

Silence fell across the table. It lasted so long, Zoe feared Romeo was upset with her.

"Honestly, I don't know. I love what I do, and I'm good at it. Most importantly, my dad is proud of me and my success. In the Italian culture, pleasing your parents is everything, and even though my old man was hard on me, I never wanted to disappoint him."

A grim expression covered his face as he spoke about his tense relationship with his father and his tumultuous childhood. Zoe's heart ached for him. She'd been raised in a loving, supportive home with parents who praised her accomplishments. Thanks to her mom and dad, she was living her dreams. Listening to Romeo talk about his background and the stress of growing up in a high-profile family, Zoe was more convinced than ever that Lizabeth had lied to the tabloids about him. She felt guilty for giving Romeo a hard time when they first met.

Zoe's thoughts returned to that fateful November morning, and she cringed. She of all people should have known better than to judge a book by its cover. Because of her dark skin and kinky hair, people assumed she was an uneducated African immigrant, often treating her with disdain. But once she spoke Italian, they sang another tune. Meeting Romeo had taught her a valuable lesson. Everyone deserved a fair shake—even dangerously handsome playboys.

Every few minutes, the waitstaff would arrive with another expertly prepared dish and their conversation would be put on hold. Dining at La Piastra Calda wasn't about the food, it was about the ambience, and Zoe enjoyed it all. Eating at the celebrity hot spot was a thrilling, exciting event, and Zoe couldn't wait to tell her sister all about her dream date with Romeo.

"Have you ever been engaged?" Romeo asked, leaning back comfortably in his chair.

Heat burned her cheeks, and her throat closed up, but she spoke in a calm voice.

"Once, but it didn't work out. He threatened to dump me if I traveled to Europe for the summer, so I broke things off." Zoe confided in him about her past relationships, was open and honest about the mistakes she'd made with her first love and her burning desire to get married and have children. She tried to gauge Romeo's mood, to figure out if her confession had turned him off, but he was a hard man to read and wore a blank expression on his face.

"I don't know if I'll ever get married or have kids," he said, shrugging his shoulder.

"But you were engaged for over a year. What happened to change your mind?"

"I proposed because it seemed like the right thing to do at the time, but my heart wasn't in it." Sadness filled his eyes, and he spoke in a somber tone. "I don't think Lizabeth was ready for marriage, either. The only thing she seemed committed to was spending my money."

They sat in silence for several seconds.

"From the moment we met, I was completely and utterly captivated by you…"

Moved by the sincerity of his voice, Zoe leaned forward in her chair, desperate to hear more.

"The more time we spend together, the more I desire you," Romeo confessed, intertwining his fingers with hers. "To be honest, these days I can't think of anything *but* you…"

Zoe's mouth dried. It was hard to breathe, to think straight when Romeo was gazing deep in her eyes and caressing her hands. Questions about the future rose in her mind, but it felt like her lips were glued together, and she couldn't pry them apart.

The waitress arrived with the final course, and Zoe had never been more relieved to see anyone in her life. The tension in the air made her temperature climb, her palms sweat, and when the lights dimmed Zoe wondered what other surprises Romeo had up his sleeve. Their conversation was getting intense, his hands too close for comfort, and if he licked his lips one more time, *he* was going to be dessert.

"We'll need to leave in the next thirty minutes to be on time for the concert."

Zoe snatched her purse off the table and rose to her feet. "Why wait? Let's go now."

"*Someone's* anxious to see Il Divo," Romeo teased.

"Damn skippy! I've been looking forward to tonight for weeks."

"Is that why you agreed to be my date? Because you have the hots for the male quartet?"

Zoe flashed an innocent smile. "I'll never tell."

Zoe sat beside Romeo in the Teatro degli Arcimboldi staring at Il Divo as they sang the last song of their three-hour concert. Mesmerized by the sound of their melodic voices, she closed her eyes and settled back comfortably in her cushy seat. The quartet was so talented, and their voices were so soulful, Zoe got goose bumps. It was an outstanding show, hands down the best concert she'd ever been to, and their heartfelt rendition of the classic Christmas song moved her to tears. Seasoned performers who'd traveled all over the world thrilling fans for years, they sang in Spanish, English and Italian, and wowed the audience with their stellar vocals and dance moves.

Applause erupted across the auditorium. Dumping her shawl on her seat, Zoe stood and cupped her hands around her mouth. She shouted louder than anyone, whistled and cheered as the quartet waved to their fans, then marched off the stage in single file.

"What do you think?" Romeo asked with a lopsided grin, hugging her to his side. "Did I get ripped off, or were our front-row seats worth every penny?"

Overcome with happiness, Zoe rested her head on his shoulder and snuggled against him. Her heart was full, bursting with joy, and she reveled in the moment and how incredible it felt being wrapped up in his arms. "Romeo, thank you for an incredible evening…"

His aftershave washed over her, derailing her thoughts, and seconds passed before she regained the use of her tongue. The oh-so-sexy tycoon was her weakness, the only man she'd ever met who made her want her to break all of the rules. It was a challenge to keep her wits about her when all she could think about was making love to him.

"This is going to go down as one of the best dates I've ever had."

"There's still more to come."

Her body tensed, and the smile slid off her face.

"Zoe, baby, relax. It's not what you think. I have a surprise for you."

Relief flooded her body, and Zoe moved toward Romeo instead of away from him. "Another one? Don't you think you've done enough? You've been spoiling me since you picked me up from my apartment. I don't think my heart can handle any more surprises tonight."

Fans streamed up the aisles to the marked exits, chatting and giggling, and Zoe wondered if she looked as exuberant as they did. Vibrating with excitement, she couldn't wait to upload her pictures of the concert on her social media sites. She knew her girlfriends in the States would be green with envy when she told them about her wonderful, magical night with Romeo.

"I've arranged for you to meet Il Divo."

"Sure you did, and I'm twenty-one!" Zoe joked.

"Baby, I'm serious. My publicist knows their manager, and she arranged everything."

Zoe stopped laughing. "Come again?"

"You'll meet Il Divo, take pictures with them and receive a swag bag filled with supercool autographed merchandise."

Before Zoe could respond, a redhead in a shapeless black gown appeared in the aisle, clutching a metal clipboard to her chest. "You must be Romeo."

"Guilty as charged," he said with a boyish smile.

"It's a pleasure to finally meet you. Giuseppe talks

about you all the time, but don't worry, I never believe anything he says."

Chuckling, he draped an arm around Zoe's waist and hugged her to his side. "Thank you so much for the meet-and-greet passes, Anna-Marie. My girlfriend is a huge Il Divo fan, and she's so excited to meet them, her hands are shaking."

Not just my hands. I'm shaking all over! Perspiration wet Zoe's forehead and trickled down the back of her designer dress. She'd never fainted before and didn't know what the signs and symptoms were, but her skin was clammy, and her head was spinning so fast Zoe feared she'd drop to the floor. Thankfully, Romeo was at her side. He gave her a reassuring smile, and the butterflies in her stomach vanished.

"Right this way. The guys are excited to meet you, so follow me to their greenroom."

The tour manager took them onstage, past the black velvet curtains and down a long, narrow corridor swarming with lighting technicians, sound engineers, service staff and suit-clad men in designer sunglasses who looked important. The air held the faint scent of roses and cigar smoke, and Zoe could hear jazz music playing in the distance. They followed the redhead into a spacious room filled with scrumptious sofas and armchairs, stained-glass windows, and the largest fish tank Zoe had ever seen. And there, standing at the bar, was her favorite group of all time. Blown away, in such a state of shock she couldn't speak, all Zoe could do was smile and nod. One by one, they hugged her and kissed her on each cheek. She felt like a ninny for clamming up and was grateful Romeo talked and cracked jokes with the group. The meet and greet was a blur, and although Zoe only said a few words, it was one of the coolest things that had happened to her since moving to Milan. They took pictures with the group, and Zoe beamed when the leader sing gave her an autographed gift bag filled with Il Divo merchandise.

"How was that?" Romeo asked as they exited the auditorium through the staff entrance. "Was the meet and greet with Il Divo everything you'd thought it would be?"

Zoe wore a sheepish smile. "Yes, but I wish I hadn't clammed up in the greenroom."

"You met your all-time favorite group. It could happen to anyone."

Taking his car keys out of his pocket, he disabled the alarm and unlocked the doors.

"I feel like such a tool," Zoe confessed, dropping her face in her hands. Pressing her eyes shut, she relived her ten-minute visit to the greenroom over and over again in her mind. "It was my chance to tell Il Divo how much I love their music, and I blew it."

Romeo opened the passenger-side door, then rubbed her bent shoulders. "You're wrong. It was obvious to everyone in the room how much you admire them, so quit beating yourself up."

Raising her head, she looked him straight in the eye, a girlish smile curling her lips.

"Is it obvious how much I appreciate you and everything you did tonight?"

Zoe draped her arms around his neck. To show Romeo how she felt about him, she closed her eyes and brushed her lips against his mouth. In that moment, standing in the middle of the Teatro degli Arcimboldi parking lot kissing her gorgeous date, Zoe had a change of heart. She wasn't going to sleep in the guest cottage at Romeo's villa. They were going to make love in his master suite, and Zoe could hardly wait.

Chapter 16

On Saturday morning, Zoe emerged from the en suite bathroom in the guest bedroom of the lavish Morretti villa feeling relaxed and carefree, even though she'd screwed up last night. *So much for a passionate night of lovemaking*, she thought, plopping down on the canopy bed to lotion her body with shea butter. She'd fallen asleep during the forty-five-minute drive to the Morretti estate. Zoe was so tired when they'd finally arrived, Romeo had to help her inside to the guest bedroom.

All wasn't lost, Zoe decided, glancing at the bronze clock on the marble end table. If she hurried, she could have everything ready by the time Romeo finished working out. A creature of habit who never skipped his morning workout, she'd bet he was already running on the treadmill or lifting weights in his home gym.

Standing, Zoe pulled on a mauve off-the-shoulder sweater and denim jeans. To make it up to Romeo for dozing off, she was going down to the kitchen to make him a breakfast fit for a king. She'd woken up an hour earlier thinking about Romeo and the Il Divo concert. Eager to tell her friends about their romantic date, she'd found her cell phone in her purse and switched it on. But it didn't work. In her haste to leave the apartment yesterday, Zoe had forgotten to pack her cell phone charger, but decided not to fret about it. She was always preaching to Romeo to take a break from his electronic devices, and it was time she took her own advice.

To clear her head, she'd treated herself to a long, luxurious bubble bath, but now that Zoe was dressed and her hair and makeup were done, she was anxious to start cooking. She put on her wedge sandals, threw open the bedroom door and hurried down the hall.

Sunlight spilled through arched windows, brightening the villa. It was surrounded by leafy trees, a vibrant landscaped garden and rolling hills, and as Zoe admired her elegant surroundings, her eyes widened. Decorated in marble and glass, with designer furniture, bejeweled chandeliers and hardwood floors so shiny she could see her reflection, she noted the twelve-bedroom villa had an Italian Renaissance ambience and more amenities than a five-star hotel.

Frowning, Zoe stopped and slanted her head to the right. She heard voices. Laughter. Someone speaking in rapid-fire Italian. She glanced around the second floor, but she didn't see anyone. Realizing the noise was coming from the end of the hall, she moved to the closed door, gripped the handle and creaked it open.

A smile warmed her mouth. Entering the lavish bedroom, which was decorated with plush carpet, scrumptious leather furniture, decorative floor lamps and an entertainment unit filled with every electronic known to man, Zoe spotted Romeo standing on the balcony talking on his cell through his earpiece and swallowed a moan. Holy heavens! What a sinfully sexy profile! Bare-chested, in nothing but a pair of black boxer briefs that fit his physique like a second skin, he reminded her of a swimsuit model. He had broad shoulders, a great butt and a pair of long, toned legs. Desire rippled across her skin.

Romeo ended his call, but as he turned away from the balcony, Zoe noticed he had a pill bottle in his right hand and a miniature needle in the other. A gasp rose in her throat, and she cupped a hand over her mouth. Zoe wanted to leave, but her legs were frozen, and her feet glued to the floor. She wanted to speak, to ask him what was going on, but her mouth didn't work.

Romeo looked up, noticed her standing beside the closet door and turned white. Guilt covered his face. He dumped the needle on the bed, but it was too late.

He reached for her, but she moved backward. For the first time, she noticed the scar on his chest that stretched from his collarbone to the top of his abs.

"Zoe, wait, it's not what you think!"

"I know what I saw. I'm not stupid."

His jaw tensed, but he spoke in a soft, quiet voice. "I have a prescription."

Wanting to be alone, she turned toward the door, anxious to return to the spare bedroom.

Moving fast, Romeo beat her to it, and slid in front of the door. "Zoe, I'm telling the truth. I swear," he said, raising his hand in the air. "Look at the vial. My doctor's name, the address of his clinic and his office number is on the label. Check it out."

The prescription was in Italian, and although Zoe could read it she didn't know what papaverine hydrochloride was, or how to pronounce it. His explanation was plausible, but she still had her doubts. "If what you're telling me is true, then why do you look so guilty?"

"I don't feel guilty." He rubbed a hand along the back of his neck. "I'm embarrassed."

"About what?"

"I wasn't trying to deceive you. I was waiting for the right time to tell you."

"Waiting for the right time to tell me what?"

Romeo looked pale, sounded breathless, unlike his cool, debonair self. "I was going to tell you before things got serious with us…" He trailed off speaking.

"Tell me what? You're talking in circles, Romeo, and I don't understand."

He gestured to the king-size bed draped in black satin, but Zoe didn't move. Couldn't. She was so upset and confused she couldn't think, let alone move, and still wanted to make a break for the door. Taking her hand, Romeo led her over to the love seat in the corner of the spacious room and sat down beside her.

Zoe had a million questions racing through her mind. Romeo owed her an explanation, and although her inner voice was screaming at her to leave, she clasped her hands in her lap and waited for him to explain what the hell was going on.

The air was charged with tension, and nervous energy filled the sun-drenched room.

Zoe didn't know how long they sat there in silence, but her anxiety increased with each passing second. How could something like this happen? Had she missed the signs? Been so smitten with Romeo and flattered by his attention that she'd ignored the obvious? Panic seized her heart. What else was he hiding from her?

"Romeo, talk to me," she pleaded. "Help me understand what's going on."

"I had a heart attack last year."

His words didn't make sense, didn't register in her brain. "But you're only thirty-two and you're healthy, fit and strong. How is that possible?"

"I've been asking myself the same thing for the past sixteen months, but I still don't have the answers, and neither does my medical team..."

Her stomach growled for food, but Zoe ignored her hunger pangs and listened to Romeo's shocking story. They were sitting side by side on the couch, but he spoke in such a quiet voice, Zoe had to strain to hear him. A muscle flickered in his jaw, and anger seeped from his pores as he opened up to her about collapsing in his home office one morning in August. He was angry at his body for failing him, for letting him down, and Zoe didn't know what to say to comfort him. Romeo praised his publicist Giuseppe Del Piero not only for saving his life, but for keeping his medical condition out of the media.

"If Giuseppe hadn't stopped by my penthouse to check on me, I wouldn't be here."

"Thank God he did," Zoe whispered, resting a hand on his leg. Romeo was a survivor, a fighter, and she'd never respected him more. He shared details about the weeks he'd spent at the private hospital and the exceptional care and support he'd received from the doctors and nurses there, but what impressed Zoe most was how his family had rallied around him. They'd dropped everything to be at his side, had flown in from all around the world to nurse him back to health, and he appreciated the sacrifices they'd made.

"How do you feel now? Have the doctors given you a clean bill of health?"

For the first time since she'd entered his room, Romeo smiled. "Yes, they have."

Perspiration dotted her forehead and clung to her sweater, but she sighed in relief.

"I take a blood thinner three times a day and give myself an injection to help lower my blood pressure so my heart and arteries can function," he explained, rubbing his eyes with the back of his hand. "I've been taking the medication since I was discharged from the hospital. I hate giving myself injections, but if I want to prevent another trip to the emergency room, I have no choice. I'll need to be on the medication for the rest of my life."

"Romeo, your story is so moving, it gave me chills," Zoe confessed. "You should share it with others. In doing so, you could save a lot of lives."

He shook his head. "I change lives by donating to charity, and that's more than enough. I'm a private person, and I don't want the whole world knowing my business."

"I know a clinical physiologist who runs a support group for people who've survived—"

"No." His voice was firm. "It's not for me. I don't want my clients or my staff to know I had a heart attack. It's humiliating, and I don't want them to think less of me."

"No one will think less of you. You're a brave and courageous man who beat the odds."

His cell phone rang, and his gaze darted around the room. Zoe wanted to keep talking, to hear more about Romeo's fears, and hoped he'd let the call go to voice mail. He did, and she smiled her thanks. Resting her head on his shoulder, she snuggled against him. She enjoyed the warmth of his touch, and his scent relaxed her.

"Thanks for sharing your story with me. It means a lot to me."

Romeo cleared his throat, then coughed into his fist. "I have one more thing to tell you."

Zoe sat up. Her body tensed, and her stomach curled into a knot.

"The doctors did a battery of tests on me, and they discovered that I'm genetically predisposed to having high blood pressure and heart failure," he explained, a pained expression on his face. "If I had children there's a fifty percent chance I could pass it on to them."

Filled with sympathy, she wore a sad smile. "Is that why you don't want to get married or have kids? Because you had a heart attack?"

"It wouldn't be fair to pass my genetic condition on to an innocent child." Exhaling deeply, he raked a hand through his short, tousled hair. "What if it happens again? What if I collapse on my wedding day? Or drop dead at my son's or daughter's youth football game?"

She cupped his face in her palms, forcing him to look right at her. "Romeo, you can't live your life in fear," she said in a soothing voice, desperate to reach him with her words. "Try not to dwell on your condition or worry about the future. Make the most of each day, and enjoy the beauty of every single moment."

Romeo covered her hand with his own and kissed her palm. "You're only thirty-two," he teased, cocking an eyebrow. "How did you become so wise at such a young age?"

"My grandmother was hospitalized in life-threatening condition a few days after I graduated from Long Island University, and one of the last things I remember her telling me was to live each day as if it were my last, because tomorrow wasn't guaranteed."

"Is that why you traveled abroad? Because you wanted an adventure?"

"Yes, and to gain some self-confidence and independence. Leaving home and everything that was familiar to me was a tough decision to make, and it cost me my college sweetheart, but if I had to do it all over again I'd make the same choice."

"One man's failure is another man's success," Romeo said with a lopsided grin.

"You are *so* wise. Do you have any other pearls of wisdom, oh smart one?"

"Obey all traffic laws. If you don't, you could get hurt."

Outraged by his joke, Zoe snatched a throw cushion off the sofa and hit him in the shoulder. "You're terrible!" she shouted, striking him again. "You should be in prison for reckless driving instead of sitting here making fun of me—"

Standing, Romeo scooped Zoe up in his arms, spun her around the room, then dropped her on the bed. It happened fast, catching her off guard, and she never saw it coming. He jumped on top of her, and Zoe burst out laughing. "You're a madman!"

"I've had enough of your mouth for one day," he growled, pinning her arms above her head, mischief glimmering in his eyes. "What am I going to do with you?"

Aroused by the huskiness of his voice and the feel of his erection against her thigh, Zoe pressed her lips to his chin, his collarbone, then along the faint scar on his chest. "I could think of a couple things, Diavolo Sexy, but you'd have to strip first."

"Last night when I picked you up from your apartment you said you weren't ready for a sexual relationship. What happened to change your mind?"

Zoe inhaled sharply. Romeo had serious baggage, and if Casa Di Moda folded in the new year, she'd be leaving Milan for good, but none of that mattered. The truth was she desired him, wanted him and was tired of fighting their attraction. Couldn't do it any longer. Zoe loved to be touched, and kissed, and held, and Romeo wasn't shy about showing his feelings. Didn't care who was around or who was watching. Zoe felt beautiful and desirable in his arms.

"Yesterday, I was scared of you hurting me by hooking up with your ex, but I'm not afraid anymore. I'm going to take my grandmother's advice and live life to the fullest, without fear."

Romeo spoke to her in Italian.

His words made her heart soft. *Beautiful, wise and sexy? Damn, you are the total package, and I'm glad you're mine, all mine.* Encouraged, Zoe nibbled his bottom lip. "We're going to make love, and it's going to be sexy and passionate and freaky."

A deep, throaty chuckle erupted from his mouth. "You are *such* a nasty woman."

Zoe winked. "Thanks, I'll take that as a compliment."

"As you should."

He slipped a hand under her bottom, cupped and massaged her ass through her jeans.

"It's obvious you're a woman of many talents, and I want to experience them all."

Draping her arms around his neck, she licked the rim of his ear with her tongue and rubbed her hips against his crotch. "Do you have protection?"

Sitting up, Romeo yanked open the top drawer of the end table beside the bed. He rummaged around for several seconds, mumbling to himself in Italian. Grinning from ear to ear, he raised his fist triumphantly in the air. "I found one!" he shouted, diving on top of her. "Buckle up, baby. I'm going to rock your world."

Laughing and kissing, they rolled around on the bed, holding each other close. Zoe was floating on air, so giddy with excitement as thoughts of making love to Romeo consumed her mind. His touch was exhilarating and thrilled every inch of her body. His hands were her downfall, her undoing. As he caressed and stroked her skin, she tingled all over.

The strangest thing happened. An intense flood of pleasure inundated every inch of her body, and a moan fell from her lips. Zoe knew it couldn't be the alcohol she'd had last night at dinner that made her feel bold but the intoxicating pleasure of his kiss. Shedding her clothes, she climbed onto Romeo's lap, and shoved him down on the bed. Eager to please, she trailed kisses along his neck. Sucked a nipple into her mouth. Rubbed his shoulders. Whispered dirty words into his ear. Took off his boxer briefs and tossed them on the floor. Seized his shaft in her hands. Watched with wide eyes and a dry mouth as it doubled in size. It was long and thick, and stroking his package excited her. Aroused her. Made her want to suck it, lick it.

Embarrassed, Zoe closed her gaping mouth. She grabbed the gold packet off the bed, opened it and rolled the condom onto Romeo's erection. Turning around so she was facing his feet, Zoe lowered her head to his lap and kissed the tip of his erection. In that moment, pleasing Romeo was all that mattered, all she cared about, and she wanted nothing more than to make him smile. Last night, he'd spent thousands of dollars on her, had spoiled her silly from the moment he'd picked her up from her apartment, and now it was her opportunity to return the favor. She wanted to show Romeo how much she desired him, craved him, and used her tongue as an instrument of pleasure.

"Zoe, you're amazing," he said in a drowsy voice, burying his hands in her hair. "Baby, keep doing what you're doing… Don't stop… Your technique is incredible…"

Encouraged by his praise, she sucked his shaft, pressed kisses along his inner thigh and licked the trail between his legs. Romeo buried his face in her butt cheeks, surprising her, and feeling his tongue against her fleshy lips caused Zoe to moan. To grip the designer bedsheets.

Her breathing was shallow and her mouth was dry, but Zoe was ready for the main event. Was desperate to feel him inside her. Sunlight shone through the windows and the balcony doors were wide open, but Zoe didn't care, refused to let her doubts and insecurities ruin the mood. It didn't matter that she didn't have the perfect body or that she wasn't a size four. Romeo was staring at her, and love shone bright in his eyes. His desire to please her was evident in his kiss, his caress, and the heartfelt words he whispered against her lips.

Careful not to lose her balance, Zoe spun around and positioned herself on his erection, but this time she had the confidence of a burlesque dancer on a Las Vegas stage.

In perfect sync, as if they'd known each other years, rather than a few weeks, they moved together as one body. His fingers were in her hair, playing with her braids, then tweaking her nipples and stroking her hips. Zoe pressed her eyes shut, tried to savor every feeling, every emotion, every sensation flowing through her.

Kissing her lips, Romeo praised her in Italian.

Tossing her head back, Zoe erupted in laughter as his words played in her mind. *I love everything about you... your inner strength, your zest for life, your keen mind, and most importantly, how fantastic your ass looks in a pair of tight blue jeans!* Their lovemaking was wild and intense, filled with playful and intimate moments, and Zoe loved everything about it. Mostly the deliciously sexy man thrusting his hips energetically beneath her.

Fireworks exploded inside her, one after another, with no end in sight. She rocked against Romeo, hard and fast, rode him like a prizewinning Thoroughbred. Couldn't stop even if she wanted to. Clutching his shoulders, she moved faster, pumped her legs harder, swiveled her hips in tight circles. He traced his tongue around her nipples, nipping with his teeth, and an orgasm with the force of a category three hurricane knocked her over and flat on her back.

"Now it's my turn." Stretching out over her, Romeo showered her face with kisses. He didn't stop there. A wicked grin worked its way onto his mouth as he thrust his erection between her legs. He pressed his lips against her neck, mashed her breasts together, squeezed her bottom, eagerly licking and sucking her earlobe. Zoe felt high, on top of the world, and wanted to experience the mind-blowing rush of having another orgasm. To make it happen, she clamped her legs around his waist and dug her nails into his butt cheeks, urging him deep inside her. Pumping his hips, he moved his body in an erotic way.

"Baby, I'm coming," she panted, bucking against him. *"Più forte! Più veloce! Sì!"*

He obliged. His thrust becoming faster, harder, he gripped her hips, then hiked her legs in the air and kissed her inner thigh. Her orgasm must have triggered his own, because his head fell forward and he released a deep, guttural groan.

Sweat coursed down his forehead and dripped from his muscled body. His breathing was so shallow, Zoe feared he'd overexerted himself and worried about his heart condition. "Baby, are you okay? I don't want you to overdo it or push yourself too hard. We have the rest of the weekend to make love," she pointed out. "Maybe we should stop and take a break."

"Hell no." He wore a lopsided grin. "I'm great. Couldn't be better. Isn't it obvious?"

Giggling, she brushed her lips against the hollow of his throat. To please him, Zoe flicked his nipple with her tongue, then sucked it into her mouth. His body tensed, going rigid and stiff. Zoe wanted to tell Romeo she loved him and wanted a future together, but her tongue was stuck to the roof of her mouth.

Rolling onto his side, he gathered her in his arms and blew out a deep breath. "You're incredible, you know that?" Romeo kissed her forehead. "If I'd known you were a sex goddess, I would have invited you to spend the weekend at my family villa the day we met!"

Zoe screamed with laughter. His toothy smile and playful banter made her crack up, and discussing what they enjoyed most about their lovemaking helped to strengthen their bond.

"Baby, sorry about this morning. I was going to get up early and make you breakfast, but Giuseppe called and I got sidetracked," he explained, holding her close to his chest. "You must be starving. What do you want for breakfast?"

"You *are* my breakfast, and if you think you can hang, I'd like some more."

In a blink, Romeo maneuvered Zoe onto her stomach, straddled her back and slapped her ass. Once, twice, three mind-blowing times. Unable to control herself, she moaned beneath him, salivating as she envisioned his erection between her legs.

"Keep talking smack, and I'll take you over my knee."

"Please do." Wearing a cheeky smile, she glanced over her shoulder and poked her butt in the air. "I told you things were going to get freaky, and I meant it, so show me what you got."

Romeo brushed his lips against her ear. "With pleasure."

Chapter 17

"We're here," the taxi driver announced. "Casa Di Moda fashion house, right, Miss?"

Zoe wanted to finish journaling about her romantic weekend with Romeo, but she dropped her notebook in her workbag, took out her wallet and paid the driver. "Yes. Thanks."

The cab was parked in front of Casa Di Moda, but there were so many people gathered on the sidewalk that Zoe couldn't open the passenger-side door. *What in the world?* she thought, peering out the window at the young, well-dressed crowd camped out at the fashion house bright and early on Monday morning. Women were waving at her and shouting in Italian, but Zoe didn't understand what they were saying. Couldn't make sense of what was going on. *Are we doing a Christmas promotion someone forgot to tell me about? A free giveaway, perhaps?*

The noise was deafening, so loud, Zoe could feel a

headache forming in her temples. If she'd known Casa Di Moda was a zoo she never would have left the comfort of Romeo's arms, and wondered if it was too late to return to the Morretti family villa. He was working from home today, and although he'd asked her to stay and keep him company, she'd kissed him goodbye and hurried to the waiting taxicab parked outside the villa. She had no choice. The Christmas Wonderland Ball was in six days, and there was so much to do before the black-tie event that Zoe had three to-do lists on her office desk. Aurora was counting on her to not only promote the holiday collection, but to also persuade her contacts in the fashion world to do a feature cover story on Casa Di Moda. Zoe didn't want to let her boss down.

Mumbling under his breath, the heavyset cab driver jumped out of driver's seat and marched around the hood of the white compact car. Waving his hands in the air, as if he were swatting a bee, he shouted at the crowd to get out of his way, then yanked open the back door.

Grateful for his help, Zoe tipped the driver and shouldered her way through the crowd. Snowflakes fell from the sky, and the crisp wind whipped her hair around her face.

"It's her! Zoe Smith! Romeo Morretti's new lady love!"

"How does it feel to be dating the most eligible bachelor in Milan?"

"Did you have fun at the Morretti family villa this weekend?"

Paralyzed with shock, Zoe froze. She could feel the blood drain from her body. Cameras flashed in her eyes, temporarily blinding her, as reporters hurled personal questions at her. *What the hell? How do they know I spent the weekend with Romeo? I never told anyone our plans, not even Jiovanni, and he's my best friend!* Willing her legs to move, she shielded her face with her hands and dashed toward the front doors.

"Welcome to Casa Di Moda, everyone! Please feel free to come inside for a tour. You can take as many pictures as you want, and interview Zoe Smith as well…"

Like hell they can! Brushing past Aurora, who looked thrilled to see the crowd of entertainment reporters and paparazzi jostling for position on the cobblestoned sidewalk, Zoe marched into the lobby, panting like a marathon runner. Decorated with tinsel, garland and Christmas-themed lanterns, the space looked festive and bright. Glass jars of different heights and shapes were filled with colorful ornaments, and the unique window display was eye-catching. The air smelled of gingerbread cookies and apple cider, but Zoe was too upset to eat and didn't want to hang out with her colleagues in the staff room.

Entering the reception area, Zoe glanced nervously around the room. There were boxes and garment bags everywhere, interns were running in every direction clutching pink invoices in their hands, deliverymen were loading their carts, and telephones rang off the hook.

"Good morning, Zoe," greeted the receptionist. "Looking great as usual. Cute dress."

"Thanks. What's going on? There's stuff everywhere," she said, gesturing to the clothes and shoes piled high on the velvet couch. "Are we doing another an online sale?"

Beaming, Aurora marched into the room chatting a mile a minute. "You don't know?"

"Don't know what?"

"Have you been living under a rock the past forty-eight hours?"

"No, my cell's dead, and I forgot my tablet in my office on Friday night," she explained. "Now, could someone tell me what's going on, because I'm clueless."

"Zoe, you broke the internet!" Aurora shrieked. "I'm so happy I could scream!"

Could scream, Zoe thought, rubbing her ears to soothe the pain. *You* just *did*.

"MilanoFashionista.com posted pictures of you and Romeo at the Il Divo concert on their social media pages on Friday night, and an hour later the Casa Di Moda website crashed."

There was no music playing, but Aurora danced around the decorative, glass table.

Zoe's cheeks burned. "There are pictures of me and Romeo online?" she croaked, a burning sensation spreading through her chest. "*Please* tell me you're joking."

Aurora took her cell out of the back pocket of her plaid high-waisted pants, swiped her finger across the screen and raised her iPhone in the air. "See for yourself."

Feeling as if her eyes were bugging out of her head, Zoe cupped a hand over her gaping mouth. There were pictures of her and Romeo eating dinner at La Piastra Calda, slow dancing at the Il Divo concert and French kissing in front of his sports car. Why didn't she realize they were being followed? How come she didn't notice paparazzi snapping pictures?

That's because you were too busy playing tonsil hockey with Romeo! teased her inner voice. *If you had kept things PG instead of pouncing on him, you wouldn't be in this mess now.*

Zoe plucked Aurora's cell out of her hand and accessed the Internet. To her surprise, the pictures were everywhere—on gossip blogs, the local newspapers, social media outlets—and seeing them filled her with shame. Not because she regretted kissing Romeo, but because she knew when he saw the photographs he'd be pissed. The last thing Zoe wanted to do was upset him. He had enough on his plate with the problems he was having at work, and she didn't want to add to his stress. Last night in bed, after making love, he'd opened up to her about his meeting with police detectives, and even though Zoe knew nothing about investment banking or money laundering, she'd encouraged him to do the right thing, no matter what. Moved by his honesty, she'd confided in him about things she'd never shared with anyone, not even her closest friends. Romeo asked her to spend Christmas Day with him, and tears had filled her eyes. Zoe was nervous about meeting his loved ones, especially since they'd only been dating for a few weeks, but since spending the day with the Morretti family beat eating a frozen dinner alone in her apartment, she'd enthusiastically agreed.

"We sold out of everything from the holiday Christmas line, and all of our boutiques reported increased sales and foot traffic. Isn't that great? We're *finally* on top where we belong!"

Zoe swallowed hard. On one hand, she was thrilled that the holiday line was a hit with consumers, but on the other hand, she was upset that someone had taken pictures of her and Romeo and posted them online. A lump formed in her throat. What would he think when he saw the photographs? Would he be disappointed that their secret was out? Would he blame her?

"I haven't told you the best part," Aurora said, her eyes wild with excitement.

Zoe braced herself for more bad news, but she couldn't think of anything worse than being secretly photographed. Burning up, she took off her green military-style jacket and draped it over her forearm. All she could think about was Romeo. Zoe wanted to call him, but since she didn't want her colleagues listening in on their conversation, she decided to wait until she got to her office to ring his cell.

"According to *Celebrity Patella* you and Romeo are Milan's newest 'it' couple, and they've nicknamed you RoZo. Cute, huh?" Aurora threw her hands around Zoe and rocked her vigorously from side to side. "I'm so happy for me! I mean, you. I'm so happy for *you*."

It was time to leave. If she didn't, Aurora would squeeze her for the rest of the morning, and she didn't want to miss her ten o'clock phone interview with *Haute Couture*. The editor was a good friend, and Zoe was looking forward to promoting Casa Di Moda's holiday line on the popular blog. Add to that, she had calls to return, press releases to write, emails to answer and a website to update. Desperate to escape her boss's clutches, she broke free of Aurora's tight, suffocating hold and moved as fast as her suede booties could take her. "I'll see you later."

On top of the world, Aurora continued speaking, chatting excitedly in Italian.

A scowl curled her lips. *Seize the moment?* Zoe repeated. *But I don't want to date Romeo in the public eye. It could ruin our relationship, and we have the most amazing bond!* Increasing her pace, she shot across the lobby, could feel her heart racing as she ran for her life.

Entering her office, Zoe dumped her handbag on her armchair, then plugged her cell into the charger. It had been one hell of a morning, and she was grateful for a few minutes of peace and quiet, but the moment Zoe sat down at her mesh armchair, her desk phone rang. She considered letting the call go to voice mail, but she was waiting to hear back from the regional manager of the Casa Di Moda boutiques in Venice about running a New Year's Eve makeover contest and snatched the receiver off the cradle. "Good morning, Zoe Smith."

"How do you do it?"

Her heart leaped inside her chest. "Do what, Romeo?"

"Make me feel better just by hearing your beautiful voice."

Coiling the phone cord around her index finger, Zoe tried to calm her nerves by taking a deep breath and slowly pushing it out her mouth. "I'm glad you're still in a good mood. I was worried you'd be mad at me when you saw the photographs of us online."

"At first I was pissed, because those sneaky paparazzi spied on us, but when my cousins and brothers called to congratulate me on dating a Caribbean bombshell, I got over it."

"Are all the men in your family charming and suave? It sure sounds like it."

"Naw, they've got nothing on me," he bragged. "Just call me Mr. Smooth."

Zoe laughed. Relieved that he wasn't upset with her, she sat back comfortably in her chair, crossed her legs and listened as he talked about his eventful morning and his phone conversation with his brother Enrique. "I'm nervous, but also really excited about meeting Enrique and his fiancée, Isabelle, tonight at Dolce Vita. What time should I be ready for dinner?"

"That's why I'm calling. We have to reschedule for next week."

Suddenly his tone was somber, and Zoe feared something was wrong.

"Baby, what is it?" she asked, straightening in her seat. "You sound worried."

"I am. I just heard back from my lawyers, and they strongly advised me to meet with French authorities. To be honest, it was an easy decision to make."

"I'm proud of you for doing the right thing." Zoe wished they were face-to-face instead of chatting on the phone, but she didn't let the distance stop her from speaking from the heart. "Once you meet with French authorities and tell them your story you'll be exonerated. I believe it with every ounce of my being, and Romeo, you should, too."

"Thanks, babe. Your support means everything to me."

Zoe stared at her desk calendar. "When are you leaving? When will you be back?"

"I'm leaving tonight after work, but I'll be back on Saturday afternoon. Just in time to escort you to the Christmas Wonderland Ball," he explained.

"Do you want me to come with you? I want to be there to support you."

"Baby, thanks for the offer, but I know you're busy getting ready for the ball, and I don't want to take you away from work. Besides, Simona's going to be interviewed as well, so we'll fly there together with my lawyers in my private jet."

Nodding, Zoe coiled the phone cord around her index finger. She'd met Simona last week when she'd dropped by Morretti Finance and Investments with lunch for Romeo, and they'd spent a few minutes talking about the weather, their plans for the holidays and their favorite Christmas foods. Simona mentioned that her boyfriend was a trained chef, and Zoe had cheered inwardly. Now she didn't have to worry about the chief operating officer putting the moves on her man.

An intern with dyed red hair appeared in the doorway holding a garment bag in one hand and a coffee mug in the other. "Can I talk to you for a minute?" she whispered, a troubled expression on her face. "It's important, and I don't know who else to ask."

Zoe nodded, then faced the window so the intern couldn't hear what she was saying on the phone. "Romeo, I have to go, but text me when you land in Paris. It doesn't matter how late. I just need to know that you arrived safely."

"Zoe, don't worry. It's a ninety-minute flight from Milan to Paris. I'll be fine."

"I know, humor me, okay?" she said with a laugh. "Have a safe trip."

"Will do. Be good while I'm away."

"I should be telling you the same thing, Mr. Smooth!"

The sound of his throaty chuckle filled the line, tickling her ear and warming her heart. Zoe dropped the receiver in the cradle and marched around her desk to find out what the intern wanted, but she couldn't wipe the smile off her face. Romeo brought out the best in her, made her feel alive, and she adored everything about him, especially his fun-loving personality. It was a challenge, because her thoughts were on Romeo and his upcoming trip to Paris, but Zoe focused intently on what the intern was saying.

"The editor from *Bellezza Moderna* magazine just called," she explained, shifting and shuffling her feet. "She wants us to send over three distinct outfits complete with accessories and shoes for their Valentine's Day issue. I just need someone to look it over before I have everything delivered to her office."

Zoe unzipped the garment bag, noticed the intern had crammed three outfits inside, and spoke in a calm but firm voice. "This is unacceptable. If you send things out haphazardly, the editor of *Bellezza Moderna* will think we don't value the dresses or this company."

The color drained from the intern's face. "I'm sorry. I didn't know. What should I do?"

"Take everything out of the bag and carefully steam each dress," she instructed, pointing to the creases on the strapless burgundy gown. "When you're finished, hang each outfit on a velvet hanger, then spray it with perfume. One outfit per bag, no exceptions."

"Can you help me?" she squeaked. "I'm scared I'm going to make another mistake."

Zoe hesitated, struggled with what to do. She had a lot on her plate, and if she helped the intern she'd be even further behind. In the two years she'd been at Casa Di Moda, she'd done it all: fetched coffee, set up props for photo shoots, grabbed lunch for her boss, and even cleaned up after office parties and industry events. Zoe loved her job and her colleagues, and since she wanted to see the intern succeed, she nodded. "Let's go. I'll teach you."

Walking down the corridor with the intern nipping at her heels, Zoe heard Christmas music playing in the distance, boisterous laughter, smelled coffee and flowers in the air. Spotting Jiovanni at the end of the hallway, she smiled and waved. Swamped at work and busy with Romeo in the evenings, Zoe hadn't seen him in days, but noticed he had a pep in his step as he swaggered toward her and assumed things were going well with his new girlfriend. The intern promised to meet Zoe in the conference room and ducked into the staff washroom.

"Hey, beautiful! How the heck have you been?" he asked, kissing her on each cheek.

"Don't ask. Things have been crazy this week, and with Christmas right around the corner they're only going to get crazier." Zoe blew out a deep breath. Just thinking about everything she had to accomplish in the next six days made her head pound, but she was determined to complete each and every task on her list. "How have you been?"

"Fantastic. I'm one step closer to launching my own clothing line, Designs by Jiovanni, and if everything goes according to plan, I'll be leaving this dump in the new year." A broad smile filled his lips. "Let's do lunch. You can tell me all about your whirlwind romance with Romeo Morretti and your romantic weekend at his villa. You *did* see something besides the inside of his bedroom, right?"

Zoe didn't like him teasing her and punched him in the arm. "That's not funny."

"It is to me!"

"Bye, Jiovanni," she said, stepping past him.

"Lunch is on me. I'll even throw in a cup of pistachio ice cream."

Zoe stopped and glanced over her shoulder. "*Now* you're talking my language. I'm in."

"Cool. I'll meet you in the lobby at noon." Jiovanni took his cell out of the back pocket of his blue jeans, and groaned. "My phone's dead, and I need to snap some pictures of the models in the outfits I'm working on for the spring collection."

"You can use my camera," she said. "It's in my office in my workbag. Go grab it."

"Thanks, Zoe, you're the best."

"I know. I'm the best thing that's ever happened to you!"

"Damn right," Jiovanni said with a laugh. "See you at lunch, Zoe. Don't be late."

Chapter 18

Hundreds of famous names from the world of fashion, entertainment, politics and business descended on one of the oldest castles in Italy on Saturday night for the fifteenth annual Christmas Wonderland Ball. Built in the thirteenth century, the stately brick building with arched windows and picturesque views had a magical, ethereal ambience. Known as the Oscars of Milan, the black-tie event was the most talked-about party of the year, and as Romeo exited the white Rolls-Royce limousine, lights flashed, paparazzi shouted his name, and reporters clutching microphones jockeyed for position on the red carpet.

Celebrities were everywhere, but when Zoe stepped out of the luxury vehicle, the crowd pressed against the metal barricades, cheering uncontrollably. Romeo didn't blame them. Stunning in a feathered burgundy gown with a dramatic train, his girlfriend seized the attention of everyone around them, even the pop stars and Hollywood actors signing autographs. Only Zoe could wear a designer gown and look relaxed and carefree. The press couldn't get enough of her. The more she smiled and waved at the crowd, the louder they chanted her name.

Hearing snickers, Romeo glanced over his shoulder to see what was making the crowd laugh. A British supermodel in a cutout dress, platform shoes and a Mohawk struck a pose. The Christmas Wonderland Ball was by invitation only, but some of the outfits on the red carpet were so outrageous, Romeo felt as if he were at a Comic-Con convention.

"I'm not trying to brag," he whispered, gazing into her eyes. "But you're the best dressed woman here tonight, bellissima, and after the party wraps up, you're mine all mine."

"Not me, *we*," Zoe corrected. "You're so handsome I can't stop staring at you..."

Her words made his chest inflate with pride. To complement Zoe's one-of-a-kind gown, he'd paired his custom-made Casa Di Moda tuxedo with a burgundy bow tie, handkerchief and leather shoes. In the limousine during the thirty-minute drive from his villa to the castle, they'd flirted and kissed. Romeo was so hot for Zoe, all he could think about was making love to her. She was the perfect distraction, just what he needed after being interrogated by authorities for three days.

Romeo considered the past seventy-two hours. Initially, he'd been reluctant to hand over his financial records or fly to the City of Lights to meet with authorities, but after talking things over with his attorney, his brothers and Zoe, he'd agreed to the interview. Markos told him not to worry, assured him that everything would be okay, but his gut feeling was that French authorities were out to get him. Through a translator, he'd vehemently defended his name. He told them the truth about his relationship with Julio Mario Domínguez, but they'd accused him of breaking the law for profit. Shocked by the crimes his client had been charged with, Romeo realized he'd never really known the Colombian businessman. He thanked his lucky stars they'd never traveled in the same social circles. The interview was a nightmare, and once authorities told him he was free to go he'd headed straight for the airport. Last night he'd returned to Milan and the first thing he'd done once his jet landed was call Zoe. On his way to his villa, he'd picked her up, and he'd been so happy to see her he'd wrapped her up in his arms, and held her tight.

"When we get back to your place it's on, so don't overdo it on the dance floor tonight." Winking, Zoe reached out and adjusted his silk bow tie. "I have something special planned for you, and you're going to need all your strength."

"RoZo, this way!"

"Smile, RoZo, the camera loves you!"

"How about a kiss? Lay one on her, Morretti. Show the world how it's done!"

Amused by the paparazzi, Romeo shook his head. Discreetly tugging his arm, Zoe raised an eyebrow, as if to ask, "What are you waiting for?" and slowly licked her lips. That was all the encouragement Romeo needed. The air crackled with energy, and adrenaline shot through his veins as their eyes bored into each other. Romeo couldn't stop staring at her lips, could almost taste them, feel them against his. "You asked for it," he warned with a knowing smile.

Tipping his head toward her, he lowered his mouth and devoured her lips. Warm and soft, they were intoxicating, and one kiss wasn't enough. Didn't satisfy him. Left him feeling horny, not satiated. Forgetting they were on the red carpet and not in the privacy of his home, he enjoyed the pleasure of her kiss, her touch, her sweet, feminine scent. His heart swelled, overflowing with love. If Zoe hadn't broken off the kiss and climbed the steps, they never would have made it inside for cocktail hour.

Entering the main floor of the castle, Romeo heard music playing and was surprised to see the Milan Children's Choir singing in front of the ten-foot Christmas tree. They sounded like angels, and seeing their adorable faces warmed his heart. The event was for a worthy cause. Romeo hoped millions of dollars was raised for the money-strapped hospital.

"Wow, I've never seen anything like this. This must be what heaven looks like..."

Over the years, Romeo had attended many Christmas Wonderland Balls, but he'd never paid attention to the decor, so listening to Zoe ooh and aah about the extravagant decorations throughout the castle made him appreciate the beauty of the venue. Satin ribbons and silver ornaments dangled from antique chandeliers. Floral arrangements were filled with amaryllis flowers, pine branches and leaves. The room was full of tea lights, fairy lights and more candles than a Catholic cathedral.

Celebrities streamed into the venue, but Romeo only had eyes for Zoe. Intertwining his fingers with hers, he led her around the room, introducing her to notable and influential guests. Servers wearing top hats and red bow ties held trays filled with champagne, cocktails and hors d'oeuvres. Romeo enjoyed sampling everything they had to offer. Anxious to hear from his attorneys, he'd hadn't eaten anything for lunch, and his stomach was groaning and growling so loud it drowned out the children's choir.

"Do you care for some Basilicata?" a waiter asked in a thick Italian accent.

Zoe frowned, and Romeo nodded to assure her the appetizer was delicious.

"Cod with fried bell peppers," he explained. "Try one. You'll love it."

As he fed Zoe appetizers from off his plate, Romeo spotted his family members sitting at the round table directly in front of the stage. He wiped his mouth with a napkin, put his empty plate on a passing server's tray and led Zoe through the jam-packed reception hall. Intent on reaching his family, Romeo marched briskly toward the stage, but stopped abruptly when Aurora threw her arms around him, hugging him as if she were stranded at sea and he was a flotation device. "Merry Christmas to you, too," he said, staring down at the exuberant designer.

"Event coordinators just told me what you did." Aurora had tears in her eyes and spoke with awe in her voice. "On behalf of everyone at Casa Di Moda, thank you for your incredible generosity. You're a modern-day saint, a dapper one, too!"

Romeo chuckled. Wanting to do something special for Zoe, he'd purchased three dinner tables in her name, and when she saw her colleagues decked out in fancy gowns and shiny tuxedos, she screamed. Romeo loved surprising her and laughed out loud when Zoe jumped into his arms and kissed him hard on the mouth. Photographers swarmed them, capturing every moment with their cameras. But Romeo didn't mind. It was a festive occasion, a night he hoped Zoe would never forget. As long as his girlfriend was happy, he was happy.

"How did you pull this off without me knowing, and why didn't you say anything?"

Romeo kissed her forehead. "Because it wouldn't be a surprise if I told you."

Staring at him for a long moment, Zoe clasped his hand and squeezed it. "You're a good man, Romeo, and meeting you last month has been one of the best things that's ever happened to me."

"Baby, I feel the same way. You're in a class all by

yourself, Zoe. A humble, beautiful soul, and if I thought you'd say yes, I'd pop the question right here, right now."

Her eyes doubled in size, and her lips parted wordlessly. His confession had taken her by surprise, but Romeo meant every word. He hated being apart from Zoe, and kept a close eye on her whenever other men were around. But he'd never felt more secure in a relationship, and loved the idea of living with Zoe in holy matrimony. Now he understood why his cousins and brothers had proposed within weeks of meeting their girlfriends. He'd found the woman of his dreams and wanted to spend his days and nights loving her, spoiling her, treating her the way she deserved. In February, Zoe was going home to visit her family for two weeks, and he was going with her. He'd sit down with Reuben Smith and ask for his daughter's hand in marriage. Once her father gave him his blessing, he was going to plan a romantic proposal for his ladylove.

Out of the corner of his eye, he noticed his sisters-in-law Jariah and Tatiyana waving frantically at him. He also saw Francesca beckoning him over, and gestured to table one. "We better go check in with my family. As you can see, they're really excited to meet you."

Releasing his hand, Zoe fluffed her hair and adjusted the bodice of her designer gown. "I'm so nervous my heart is racing. Gosh, I hope they like me."

"What's not to like?" To make her laugh and to calm her nerves, he wiggled his eyebrows made a funny face. "You're gregarious, witty, and you have great taste in men. Baby, you've got this, so let's go wow my family!"

As they approached table one, Romeo sent Zoe a reassuring smile. She looked tense, as if she were at the dentist's office rather than a black-tie party. Placing a hand on her lower back, he gently caressed her skin. Diamonds were draped from her ears, neck and wrists, and her jewelry twinkled in the candlelight. Awed by her beauty, he was shocked that his girlfriend suddenly lacked self-confidence.

"Are you going to stand there like a well-dressed mime for the rest of the night, or are you going to introduce us to your lovely date?"

The sound of Dante's voice jolted Romeo back to the present, and he broke free of his thoughts. Pleased to see everyone, he glanced around the table. The newlyweds, Markos and Tatiyana, were busy kissing, Enrique and Isabelle were feeding each other olives, Francesca and her blonde, blue-eyed boyfriend were arguing in Italian, and Dante and his wife, Jariah, who was six months pregnant, were whispering to each other.

Thrilled to have Zoe on his arm, he proudly introduced her to his family members. To make her feel more comfortable, he shared funny stories about each couple, and soon everyone was laughing. Romeo pulled out her chair, then sat down beside her.

"Oh my goodness," Zoe shrieked, touching a hand to her mouth. "You're all wearing something from Casa Di Moda's holiday line. How cool is that!"

Enrique wore a wry smile. "We had no choice. Francesca and our sister-in-law Paris both decided to invest in the fashion house. They said if we didn't buy something they'd kill us. Needless to say, it was an easy decision to make."

"I had no idea," Zoe said with a laugh, giving Francesca a one-arm hug. "Why didn't you say anything when we met for sushi the other night?"

"Because I wanted it to be a surprise. Aurora and Davide asked if I'd be interested in being the face of the line, and I said hell yes! Thanks to you, Zoe, my life has meaning and purpose again. I'm going to make the most of this incredible opportunity…"

Romeo watched his sister and his girlfriend embrace.

He hadn't seen Francesca this excited in years, and he hoped resurrecting her modeling career and working for Casa Di Moda would help ease the pain of Lucca's death. Since losing her only child, she'd been angry at the world, but if anyone could turn their life around it was his sister. To stand out among the crowd, she'd styled her silky shoulder-length hair in a bouffant and donned a shimmery gold gown that clung to her skin like Saran Wrap. Romeo wouldn't be surprised if he woke up tomorrow morning to find Francesca on the cover of every online fashion magazine and blog in the country.

The mood at table one was cheerful and festive, the conversation lively. Romeo could tell by the way Zoe interacted with his family members that she was having a good time. The celebrity hosts entertained diners throughout the five-course meal. Soon Romeo's jaw ached from laughing, and his stomach was filled to the brim. Spending time with his family helped him momentarily forget the relentless questioning he'd endured in Paris hours earlier and his fears of being charged with a crime he didn't commit.

"RoZo, how did you meet?" Tatiyana asked, with a smile. "Was it love at first sight?"

A grin dimpled his cheek. "Absolutely. Zoe wanted to meet me so bad she drove her mountain bike into the side of my Lambo."

Zoe kicked him under the table, but Romeo was determined to finish his story.

"The police wanted to charge her with reckless driving, but I convinced them not to," he said, popping his collar to earn a laugh. "An amazing first kiss, and the rest is history."

Everyone at the table cracked up except Zoe, and Romeo wondered if he'd gone too far.

"You forgot the part about trying to pay me off and

begging me relentlessly for a date," Zoe quipped, wearing a cheeky grin. "No worries, I'll save that titillating story for dessert."

His brothers chuckled, the women gave one another high fives, and Zoe winked at him. Romeo couldn't contain his laughter. He loved her wit, and he enjoyed listening to her joke around with his family.

Francesca cupped a hand around her ear. "Anyone else *hear* wedding bells?"

"Come on, you guys." Zoe wore a shy smile. "We've only been dating for a few weeks. Hardly long enough to be thinking about marriage—"

Interrupting, the women all spoke at once. By the time they were finished telling Zoe about their whirlwind romances and lightning-fast engagements she looked stunned, as if she'd never heard anything more shocking in all her life.

"Wow," fell from her lips for the umpteenth time, and everyone laughed.

"Zoe, are you spending Christmas Day with us?" Jariah asked, rubbing her baby bump.

"Yes, and I'm really looking forward to it. My family's in New York, so it'll be nice to celebrate the holidays with you guys." Zoe picked up her flute. "Romeo promised to make me homemade ravioli with garlic focaccia, and I can't wait to try it. It's my favorite dish."

"Great!" Isabelle said with a cheer, her auburn curls tumbling around her forehead. "We're going to have so much fun. We'll open gifts, eat brunch, sing Christmas carols around the piano, then eat some more!"

Feeling his cell phone vibrate inside his jacket, he took it out of his pocket and saw Simona's number on the screen. He wondered if his COO had an update about the money laundering investigation. She'd remained in Paris, but had promised to touch base with him before she left for her family ski trip in the morning. "I need to take this," he said, wearing an apologetic smile. "I'll be right back."

Standing, Romeo pressed his cell to his ear and marched out of the reception hall. Noisy and crowded, the lobby was filled with so many people he couldn't hear himself think. Needing privacy, Romeo breezed past the fashionable group and ducked inside the men's washroom. "Have you heard from our attorneys? Are the French authorities going to press charges?"

"No, thank God," Simona said, releasing a sigh. "I found out from our attorneys that Markos called the lead investigator this afternoon, and had a lengthy conversation with him…"

Filled with relief and gratitude, Romeo nodded his head as she spoke. Markos never told him about his conversation with French authorities, but he wasn't surprised by what his brother had done. That was the Morretti way. Like the rest of his family, he had his back. Romeo could always count on Markos.

"I don't know what your brother said to get French authorities off our backs, but Markos came through for us big time. The next time I see him I'm going to give him a big fat kiss!"

"Please don't. His wife will go ballistic, and I don't want you to get hurt."

"Thanks for the heads-up. I'll just send him a Christmas fruit basket and call it a day."

They laughed, and for the first time since he'd learned about the arrest of Julio Mario Domínguez, he felt calm; he could finally breathe.

"Simona, I have to go. I'm at the Wonderland Ball with my family. They'll kill me if I spend the rest of the night on my cell," he explained, checking his reflection in the mirror.

"No worries. I understand. Merry Christmas, Romeo. Take care."

"Thanks, Simona," he said, adjusting his crooked bow tie. "Happy holidays. Have fun skiing with your sisters in Val Thorens tomorrow. Be careful. Don't break anything."

Simona giggled. "I'll try not to. See you in the New Year."

A man of African descent with lifeless eyes and pock-marked skin emerged from the handicapped stall and approached the sink.

Eager to share his good news with his family, and thank Markos for his help, Romeo turned to the door.

"For two hundred million euros, no one ever has to know about your massive heart attack last year or your weekly papaverine hydrochloride injections…"

Romeo stopped. The room spun around him at a hundred miles an hour, then flipped upside down on its head. His knees buckled, but he faced his tormentor. Took a good look at the creep who was blackmailing him. Over six feet tall, with a lanky frame hidden under a weathered, black trench coat, Romeo knew the stranger was no match for him. One punch and he'd be flat on his back, sleeping like a baby. Filled with anger, he struggled to control his temper. He was at an A-list party, crawling with reporters and paparazzi, and since Romeo didn't want to do anything to embarrass himself or his family, he kept his cool.

The stranger moved toward him wearing a menacing expression on his face, and Romeo curled his hands into fists. His tuxedo felt tighter than a straitjacket, and his bow tie was cutting off his air supply. But he was ready for war. If the man touched him it was on. He'd kick his ass like he stole something, then worry about the consequences later.

"Take this," the stranger instructed, holding up a white business card. It had a row of numbers written in black ink.

The man gestured to it with a flick of his head. "Deposit the money into this account by midnight."

Romeo spoke through clenched teeth. "And if I don't?"

"Your secrets will be published online for the whole world to read." He wore a smug smile. "I wonder what your celebrity clients will think when they find out about your ties to organized crime?"

Rage boiled inside him, causing his entire body to quiver. A minute ago he was relieved that French authorities weren't going to charge him with money laundering, and now he was stuck in the men's room, face-to-face with the devil. When was he ever going to catch a break? Refusing to feel sorry for himself, he shrugged. "I'm not giving you shit."

The man rocked on his heels, as if he'd been slugged in the stomach. "S-S-She said you'd pay. That you'd do anything to keep the story out of the papers."

"Publish whatever you want. I don't negotiate with criminals, and I don't give a—"

A British pop band, their bodyguards, and a wave of cigarette smoke filled the room. Thinking fast, Romeo slipped through the open door and out into the lobby. His heart was racing, pounding out of control. Romeo didn't know why he thought he could have a successful relationship. He'd had bad luck with the opposite sex all his life, but he'd hoped things would be different with Zoe. But like all the women in his past she'd played him, and he hadn't even seen it coming. Had never guessed in a million years she'd break his heart.

Questions bombarded his mind. Played in his ear like a bullhorn. Was Zoe dating the man in the trench coat behind his back? Had they plotted together to ruin him? He couldn't quiet his thoughts, didn't know what to believe or think, and feared the woman he'd fallen hard for had plotted his demise. *Why?* he wondered. *Why would Zoe hurt me like this?*

Desperate to reach his family, Romeo marched through the reception hall, oblivious to the world around him. Ignored the partiers smiling, waving and shouting his name. Spotting Zoe standing at the dessert table with Isabelle and Francesca, conflicting emotions flooded his body. Sadness, confusion, hurt and love. His tongue felt heavy, his throat tight. Grabbing her arm, he led her to a quiet corner of the room, away from the crowd and demanded answers. The music was loud, and Romeo had to shout to be heard over the R&B singer crooning onstage.

"What did you do?" he asked, glaring at her. "Who's the guy in the trench coat? Are you guys lovers? Why did you tell him about my heart attack?"

Frowning, Zoe reached for him, but he pushed her hands away. "Romeo, calm down. What are you talking about? You're not making any sense."

"Someone just threatened to post my health problems online if I don't pay him millions of dollars."

Her eyes widened, and her mouth fell open.

"Answer me, Zoe. What did you do?"

"I didn't do anything. I swear. I never told anyone about our conversation. I wouldn't."

"Did you hear what I just said?" he shouted, pointing at the doors. "A guy just tried to shake me down in the men's room. He knew about my heart attack, the medication I'm on, and the money laundering case."

Blinking rapidly, Zoe fervently shook her head, her earrings swishing back and forth as she denied the accusations. "I never said a word. Baby, you have to believe me. I'd never betray you like that. Not for any amount of money."

Francesca tried to talk to him, but Romeo ignored her. He was so riled up about his conversation with the man in the trench coat, he was shouting. "You did it. You screwed me over. I know you did. You betrayed me for two hundred million dollars—"

"I-I-It wasn't me," she stammered, her voice low and strained, as if it were painful for her to talk. "It could have been Lizabeth, or Giuseppe or someone who's jealous of you…"

"Lizabeth and I weren't together at the time I was hospitalized, and Giuseppe would never sell me out. Not for any amount of money. He's my mentor, and I trust him explicitly."

"And you don't trust me?"

Her gaze bored into him. His tongue stuck to the roof of his mouth, and his feet were glued to the floor. He couldn't escape even if he wanted to. And he did. Desperately. He wanted to get far away from the man in the trench coat and the partygoers dancing around them. "No. I don't. Not anymore," he said, burying his hands in his pockets to avoid reaching out to wipe the tears from her eyes. She'd betrayed him, but it hurt Romeo to see the woman he loved cry, made him feel like the scum of the earth even though he'd done nothing wrong. As much as he didn't want to believe it he couldn't ignore the facts: he and Zoe were over.

Needing to be alone and anxious to leave the party, he searched for his brothers. Zoe touched his forearm, warming his chilled body, but he hardened his heart. Told himself she was no longer worthy of his love. That she was his past, not his future, and she never would be.

"Romeo, *non farlo*," she pleaded, wiping at her eyes with the back of her hands. Zoe spoke in Italian, but he didn't believe her, couldn't look at her.

Her words blew his mind. *Don't do this? We can fix this. We can work things out.*

"Work what out? There is no us. You ruined us when you betrayed me."

"Stop saying that! I never told anyone about your health issues. Not even my sister."

"Then how the hell does that scumbag know about the worst day of my life?"

Zoe hugged her arms to her chest. Tears dribbled down her cheeks, running the expensive makeup she'd spent an hour putting on in his master bathroom as he'd gotten dressed for the Wonderland Ball. She was shaking so violently, Isabelle had to come to her aid. He didn't know how much of his argument with Zoe family members had heard, and didn't want to put them in the middle of his relationship dispute, but he needed their help.

"Francesca, see to it that Zoe gets home safe," he whispered in her ear. "Please? As a favor to me? I need to be alone right now. I can't be here. I need to go."

"I understand. I will." Francesca kissed his cheek. "I love you, bro. Take it easy."

Romeo turned and walked out of the room, but as he pushed open the glass door he noticed he wasn't alone. His brothers were beside him, shoulder to shoulder. For as long as Romeo lived, he'd never forget the night they'd sacrificed time with their wives to comfort him.

The air was crisp and cold; the wind was howling, the ground now covered in snow. Ducking inside the limousine parked at the front entrance of the castle, Romeo collapsed into the backseat and yanked off his bow tie. Tossing it on the floor, he stretched his legs out in front of him. He tried to block out the noises in his head, the memory of his argument with Zoe, but he couldn't do it. Pressing his eyes shut, he prayed when he woke up he'd discover that the Christmas Wonderland Ball had been nothing more than a bad dream, and the vivacious Long Island beauty he adored in every way was still his ladylove.

Chapter 19

Zoe yanked open the front door of Casa Di Moda so hard she was surprised it was still on its hinges. The burly security guard with the thick beard must have seen the peeved expression on her face, because he moved out of her way and took cover behind a leafy, potted tree.

Stomping through the darkened reception area, her suede over-the-knee boots slapping against the floor, she struggled to control her emotions, the sadness and anger pulsing through her veins. Zoe had never experienced such pain in all her life, and every time she remembered what happened at the Christmas Wonderland Ball on Saturday night she'd break down. Couldn't help it. Couldn't stop the tears from falling once they started. She'd tell herself to toughen up, but she didn't have the strength it required.

Each day without Romeo was unbearable. It had only been four days since he'd dumped her, but it felt like months had passed since she'd seen the man she loved.

Stuck in her apartment, listening to sad love songs only made her feel worse, but Zoe didn't know what to do to get out of her funk.

For days, she'd mentally reviewed their argument, analyzing everything he'd said and done at the party. That morning, while Zoe was curled up in bed looking at pictures of Romeo on her cell phone, she'd realized she'd overlooked something important. Something she should have told Romeo before he stormed off. She never told anyone what he'd told her about his health issues, but she'd journaled about it in the taxicab after their first weekend together at the villa on her way to work.

A light bulb had gone off in her head. Scrambling to her feet, she'd jumped out of bed, grabbed her leather tote bag from the closet and opened it. To her surprise, her journal was inside. Flipping through it, she noticed all of the pages were intact, and her owl-shaped bookmark was right where she'd left it.

Disappointed, she'd slumped to the floor, striking the carpet with her fists. She'd thought her journal was stolen, was convinced someone had taken it from her purse when she'd gone Christmas shopping with Francesca or to the movies with Jiovanni, just days before the Wonderland Ball. Finding it meant she was back to square one.

Another thought had come to her. Had one of her colleagues read her journal, then hired someone to blackmail Romeo? It was hard to believe, but the more Zoe considered it, the more plausible it was. She had great relationships with her colleagues and couldn't imagine any of them snooping through her things, but she couldn't rule it out, either.

Who would do something so sinister? So cruel, she'd wondered, racking her brain. Who had motive? Opportunity? A desire for fame and fortune that rivaled a reality

TV star? A chilling thought rocked her mind. Conversations she'd had with Aurora in recent weeks blared in her ears. *Romeo Morretti's a smart, influential businessman with friends in high places, and we could use someone like him in our corner... Hooking up with a Morretti is a once-in-a-lifetime opportunity, so don't blow it... Do whatever it takes to persuade him to invest in Casa Di Moda... I'll do anything to save Casa Di Moda. It's my life, and I won't lose it.*

Convinced she finally knew who the guilty party was, Zoe had tossed her journal aside, surged to her feet and marched into the bathroom to shower and change. An hour later, a taxicab had dropped her in front of Casa Di Moda. The office was closed for the holidays, but Zoe knew Aurora was hard at work on the spring collection. Zoe wasn't leaving the fashion house until the cold and callous designer answered her questions.

Heading toward her boss's large corner office, her anger intensified. Obsessed with fame and fortune, Aurora would do anything to achieve her goals—including stabbing her in the back and destroying the best relationship Zoe had ever had. Hell, she'd probably fake her own death and collect the insurance money if she thought she could get away with it, Zoe thought. *I can't believe I ever considered Aurora a friend!*

Seeing the Christmas wreath hanging on the staff room door reminded Zoe of the plans she'd made with Romeo and his family for the holidays. Plans she was now excluded from. Zoe never imagined she'd be at Casa Di Moda on Christmas Eve, instead wishing she was with Romeo and his family at the Milan Christmas parade. Last night she'd reached out to Francesca, and to her surprise and relief, she agreed to talk to Romeo on her behalf. It was the best news she'd received all week, and even though Francesca told her not to get her hopes up, Zoe was praying for a Christmas miracle.

"Davide, what should I do? Should we tell Zoe the truth or wait..."

Zoe stopped. Hearing voices coming from the end of the hall, she spun around and peeked inside the staff room. And there, sitting at the round table sipping coffee and eating cookies, were Aurora and Davide. Sketchbooks, file folders, fashion magazines and vibrant silk fabric were spread out in front of them. But it was obvious they were relaxing not working. Italian music was playing on the stereo, and the festive up-tempo song only made Zoe feel worse about being alone on Christmas Eve.

Something snapped in Zoe, and as she stormed over to the table she shouted her words. "Aurora, how could you do this to me? To Romeo? Don't you have a heart? Don't you care about anybody but yourself?"

The couple stared at her, their mouths ajar.

"I helped you, supported you, did everything in my power to promote Casa Di Moda, and how do you repay me? By betraying me. How could you?"

Aurora dropped her utensils on her plate, wiped her mouth with a red star-shaped napkin and rose to her feet. "I saw the articles online about Romeo's health crisis, but I had nothing to do with it. I didn't even know he was sick," she said quietly, meeting her gaze. "You're important to me, Zoe, and I'd never do anything to hurt you. Neither would Davide."

Biting the bottom of her lip, Zoe stared down at her boots. For some strange reason, she believed her. Knew in her gut that Aurora was telling the truth. That her boss didn't sell the story to the press her.

"You helped us save Casa Di Moda, and we're forever in your debt. You're our family, Zoe, and we'd never do the things you're accusing us of. How could we? If not for you and the rest of our amazing staff, we would have lost everything." Standing, his arms outstretched, Davide crossed the room toward her. "We'll get through this together. I promise."

The couple wrapped their arms around her. Zoe's throat closed up and water filled her eyes, blurring her vision. She felt guilty for yelling at her boss, ashamed of herself for ever thinking that Aurora and Davide would screw her over. She quickly apologized for her assumptions.

Davide wore a sympathetic smile. "Don't sweat it. We all make mistakes."

"Romeo dumped me," she croaked, wiping her eyes with the sleeve of her beige cardigan. "He thinks I released information about his health…but I didn't…now he hates me."

Aurora cupped Zoe's face in her hands. "Don't talk like that. Romeo's just upset. Give him time. Once the media storm dies down, he'll realize breaking up with you was a mistake."

"When? He won't take my calls or respond to my texts. It's killing me inside."

"Don't worry, Zoe. He'll come to his senses. Romeo loves you, and he wants a future with you," Davide said with assurance. "I know it's hard, but be patient with him. He's going through a lot right now. I bet he's just as upset as you are."

Zoe considered Davide's words and smiled through her tears. "Look at me, I'm a mess."

"You sure are!" Aurora said, making a face. "You better hurry up and get yourself together because time is of the essence. Your goddaughter will be here in five months, and I'm going to need your help."

Davide sighed, as if he had the weight of the world on

his shoulders, then wore a sheepish smile. "Me, too. I know zilch about babies, and even less about changing diapers!"

A feeling of elation came over Zoe, and she let out a scream. "You guys are pregnant?"

"No, not me. Just Aurora," Davide joked, touching his wife's stomach. "Our little bundle of joy should be here by May. Just in time for my fortieth birthday. Pretty cool, huh?"

"Congratulations, you guys! I'm so happy for you." Hugging them both, she decided it was cause for celebration and offered to buy them lunch at the bistro across the street.

"We should be the ones spoiling you. You saved Casa Di Moda from financial ruin."

I did? Zoe thought, bewildered by Aurora's words.

"Thanks to you, the Chic and Curvy line is our best-seller," Davide explained.

"The fashion blogs can't get enough of your effortless style, and we've seen a three hundred percent surge in online sales since you were photographed with Romeo at the Il Divo concert," Aurora said, putting on her belted tweed jacket. "I call it the Zoe Effect, and our increased popularity and staggering profits are making our new investors very happy."

"I'm glad that everything worked out. You're an incredible talent, Aurora, and you deserve every bit of success," Zoe said. "I just know you're going to be an amazing mom."

"Damn right. My daughter's going to be the best-dressed kid in preschool!"

Laughing, the trio left the staff room, their exuberant voices carrying down the hall. It had been days since Zoe smiled or joked around. She missed Romeo desperately and longed to see him again, but she was glad she could spend some quality time with her boss.

Remembering she'd bought Christmas presents for Romeo's family and stashed them under her office desk, Zoe asked Davide to help her carry them to the reception area and opened the door. Her purse fell from her hands, and everything inside spilled onto the carpet. *Is this really happening?* she wondered, giving her head a shake to clear the terrifying image before her eyes. *Is my best friend stealing from me? Is Jiovanni the one who stabbed me in the back?*

Zoe forced herself not to cry. He'd always had a word of encouragement for her, had always been her biggest cheerleader. His betrayal cut deep. It felt as if there were a hole in her chest where her heart should have been, but she didn't succumb to her pain. For the first time since the Christmas Wonderland Ball, her mind was clear. In that moment, Zoe realized everything her colleagues had said about Jiovanni over the last few months was true. He was angry and bitter, and if he was her friend he wouldn't be standing behind her desk, snooping through the gifts she'd bought for Romeo's family. "Looking for something? My journal perhaps?"

His head snapped up, and he dropped the diamond earrings he was holding on the desk.

"It was you," she hissed, pointing a finger at his face.

"Z-Z-Zoe, what's up? I just came by to grab the issue of *Vogue* I lent you."

"Liar! You read my journal, then arranged to have some low-life criminal blackmail Romeo at the Wonderland Ball, knowing full well he'd blame me."

"Don't make it sound so sinister," he said with a shrug. "It wasn't like that."

"I thought we were friends. I thought you cared about me—"

"I do," he said, interrupting her. "It wasn't personal. Alessandra and I saw an opportunity to make some easy cash and we took it. You of all people know how much I want to launch my own fashion label."

Feeling woozy, as if she was about to be sick, Zoe took a deep breath, willed herself not to lose it.

"Alessandra and I sold the story to our favorite celebrity blog, and now I finally have enough money to fulfill my lifelong dream."

"Get out before I throw you out," Aurora warned, stepping forward. "People like you make me sick. You'll do anything for money, but what you fail to realize is when you hurt people in your quest for success, you'll never get ahead."

"Bullshit. It's the survival of the fittest in the fashion world, and only the strongest survive."

Davide gestured with his thumb to the open door. "Jiovanni, you're fired. Leave now or the security guards will escort you out. It's your choice."

"With pleasure. I was going to quit after the holidays, so thanks for saving me the trouble of having to write a formal resignation letter." Wearing a confident smile, he swaggered through the office. "I'm debuting my collection, Designs by Jiovanni, during Milan Fashion Week and it's going to mop the floor with Casa Di Moda. You just wait and see."

"Boy, bye!" Flapping her hands in the air as if she were a queen on her throne, Aurora narrowed her gaze. "You're not welcome here anymore, so please leave."

Jiovanni stopped in front of Zoe, but she stepped back. She couldn't stand to be near him.

"I know you're upset, and you have every right to be, but I hope one day you'll find it in your heart to forgive me," he said in a sincere tone of voice.

Zoe scoffed, couldn't believe his nerve. "Don't hold your breath."

"I messed up. I'm man enough to admit it. Doesn't that count for something?"

"Stay away from me. Don't call me, don't text me, don't come by my apartment. In fact, lose my number permanently."

"Zoe, you don't mean that. We're best friends. I love you. You know that."

Jiovanni reached out to touch her face, and Zoe slapped his arm so hard a sharp pain shot through her wrist. "Don't touch me. Don't you dare touch me," she hissed through clenched teeth. "Stay. The. Hell. Away. From. Me. Or. You'll. Be. Sorry."

His cheeks paled. He started to speak, but Zoe gave him her back, keeping her gaze fixed on the picture of her family hanging on the wall. What bothered her more than anything was his cocky, self-righteous attitude. Had he ever cared about her? Had he been screwing her over from day one? Filled with a profound sense of sadness, as if she were all alone in the world, Zoe bit the inside of her cheek to keep the tears at bay.

Jiovanni mumbled an apology, but Zoe refused to acknowledge him.

Out of the corner of her eye, she saw her ex-best friend leave her office, his shoulders bent, his head down, and wondered if his outward show of remorse was genuine or just an act. Deciding it was the latter, she stared out the window. She needed a moment to collect her thoughts. Zoe couldn't believe she'd lost her boyfriend and her best friend in the same week. She dropped into her favorite chair, and tears flowed fast and furious down her cheeks. It didn't matter how hard she tried, she couldn't make them stop.

Chapter 20

"Uncle Romeo, wake up, wake up, it's Christmas Day!" Matteo wailed in a high-pitched voice. "You have to come downstairs, uncle. Everyone's waiting. Santa came, and it's time to open presents!"

Groaning, Romeo buried his head under a pillow. Warm and cozy in his king-size bed, he didn't want to leave the comfort of his master suite. He silently wished Dante would come and collect his loud, hyper son. The tantalizing aromas of sausage, mozzarella cheese and sautéed mushrooms filled the air. Even though Romeo was starving, he still didn't budge. Exhausted and desperate for more sleep, he closed his eyes.

"Please, Uncle Romeo?" Matteo begged, vigorously shaking Romeo's shoulders.

"I'll be up in an hour, li'l man. I promise."

"No, get up now. I'm tired of waiting. You've been sleeping forever."

Rolling onto his side, he peered at the alarm clock on the side table. Six forty-seven a.m.? Oh, hell no! Yesterday, his nonna had arrived from the States with his cousins Demetri, and Rafael, and their wives and children. After the kids went to bed, the adults had stayed up late into the night, drinking homemade wine, eating savory snacks and sharing their favorite Christmas memories. Unfortunately, conversation had turned to Romeo's love life, and to his shock and dismay, his sisters-in-law didn't like how he'd treated Zoe. The women were disappointed in him for yelling at her at the Christmas Wonderland Ball. Francesca was convinced Zoe had nothing to do with the blackmail scheme and encouraged him to reach out to her. On the fence about what to do, he'd promised to give some thought to what his sister said, and he had. In fact, he'd thought about Zoe all night. That's why he didn't have the energy to get out of bed now.

"I'm going to tell Auntie Cesca you're being mean to me," Matteo said in a wobbly voice, jumping to his feet. "You're going to get it!"

Feeling guilty for upsetting his nephew, Romeo decided to take the first grader for a ride in his red Ferarri after breakfast. Images from his dream played in his mind, and a lump formed inside his throat. Zoe was goofing around with him at his estate in Lake Como, frolicking and laughing in the turquoise-blue water. Memories of all the good times they had over the past few weeks made his heart sad.

Romeo couldn't quiet his thoughts, couldn't change the channel in his mind. Since the Wonderland Ball, her words had haunted him. *I didn't do anything. I swear...I never told anyone about our conversation. I wouldn't...I'd never betray you...* Did he make a mistake? Had he lashed out at the wrong person? Had someone else in his inner circle sold him out? Did it even matter now that everyone knew about his health problems?

Remembering the headlines splashed across every magazine in the country gave him pause. Romeo Morretti Health Crisis! one paper had written. Morretti Millionaire Found Unresponsive at Lavish Penthouse! claimed another one. On the Brink of Death, reported his favorite newspaper.

Considering everything that had happened since the story broke five days earlier, Romeo realized he'd been worried for nothing. The response from his clients, friends and business associates had been overwhelmingly supportive. All week, he'd been bombarded with phone calls, text messages and emails. Everyone told him how brave he was, called him an inspiration, a survivor. He'd been wrong. No one thought less of him or made him feel weak. Giuseppe persuaded him to share his story with the world. Now Romeo had so many speaking engagements lined up in the new year, he'd have to reschedule his birthday trip with his brothers and cousins to Monte Carlo in January. The Heart Disease Foundation of Milan had reached out to him about filming a public service announcement. After discussing it with his family, he'd agreed. He'd taped it yesterday in his home office, and within hours of the PSA being posted on the foundation's website, it had over two million views. Filming the commercial, speaking openly and honestly about his heart attack last year, had been cathartic. The weight he'd been carrying on his shoulders disappeared. For the first time since Romeo had been discharged from the hospital, he felt at peace with his body.

Romeo heard laughter, lively Christmas music and animated voices echoing throughout his estate. There were so many people at his house it was noisier than an amusement park, but Romeo was glad his relatives were with him. He cherished the time they spent together, loved hanging out with his cousins and brothers, and was thrilled they'd be in Milan until the new year, especially now that he didn't have Zoe by his side. The unthinkable had happened: he'd found the woman of his dreams and lost her in the blink of an eye, through no fault of his own.

Yawning, he stretched his tired muscles. It had been a year of extreme highs and lows, but despite everything that had happened with Zoe at the Wonderland Ball, she was still the woman he wanted. The object of his affection. His heart. His everything, and he couldn't help wondering who she was spending Christmas Day with. Was she with Aurora and Davide? Hanging out with Jiovanni and his family? Or relaxing at home watching her favorite Christmas movie for the hundredth time?

High heels slapped against the marble floor, echoing throughout the second story, ruining the peaceful mood. Romeo cursed under his breath. Sensing what was coming next, he threw the blanket over his face and pretended to snore.

"Get up, sleepyhead!" Francesca trilled in a singsong voice. "Everyone's waiting for you downstairs, and they're starting to get restless, so shake a leg."

Romeo grunted, blew deeply through his nose to sell his performance.

"I told you, Auntie Cesca. He's not listening," Matteo whined.

"We'll see about that."

Romeo held his breath, prayed his sister wouldn't do anything crazy like jump on his bed or worse, toss a bucket of ice water on him. Someone yanked off his blanket, stole his pillow, and whacked him upside the head with it. Squinting, he propped himself on his elbow to see who the culprit was. The blinds were drawn, the balcony doors were open, and the crisp morning air made his body cold.

Francesca stood at the foot of the bed, licking a candy cane, a hand stuck to her hip. "Are you going to come willingly, or do we have to drag you out of the bed?"

"Merry Christmas to you, too, sis," Romeo drawled in a sleepy voice, patting back a yawn. "Go ahead and start without me. I don't mind."

"Nice try, Scrooge, but that's not a Morretti family tradition. On Christmas Day, we open presents together, eat brunch, then sing Christmas carols around the piano."

Deciding to have a little fun with his sister and nephew, he shook his head and faked a scowl. Stretching out, Romeo clasped his hands behind his head and crossed his legs at the ankles. "My house, my rules, so bounce. I'll be down in an hour, and if you don't like it that's too bad."

"Come on, Matteo. Let's get him. I'll grab one leg, you grab the other!"

Before Romeo knew what was happening, Francesca and Matteo had dragged him off the bed. He fell flat on his back and let out a groan. Giggling, his nephew pointed at him with one hand and cupped his mouth with the other. Caught off guard by the surprise attack, Romeo didn't know whether to laugh or to cry.

"I'm going to get even when you least expect it, so you better watch your back!" he warned, hurling a pillow across the room. It hit the wall with a thud, and Matteo laughed even harder.

"You can't catch us. You can't catch us," the first grader chanted, wiggling his hips.

Crossing her arms, Francesca tapped her red-heeled pumps impatiently on the floor, her gaze dark and narrow. "I'd like to see you try. Now get up, get dressed and come downstairs pronto or we'll be back. The next time we won't go easy on you."

"Yeah," Matteo shouted, his curls tumbling around his face as he nodded his head. "I got a Super Soaker water gun from Nonna yesterday, and I'm not afraid to use it."

Giggling uncontrollably, Francesca and Matteo fled the room. Romeo wore a wry smile. Worried they'd return and make good on their threat, he dragged himself to his feet, shuffled into the bathroom and locked the door. A quick shower and shave, and Romeo was ready.

Jogging down the staircase, whistling "I'll Be Home for Christmas," he decided to call Zoe after breakfast. Romeo didn't know if they'd ever get back together, but he wanted to clear the air and apologize for the way he'd behaved at the Wonderland Ball. He'd been hurt and confused, but that was no excuse for his behavior. Romeo considered phoning her now, but since he didn't want Matteo to drench him with his water gun, he changed his mind.

"I'm here," Romeo announced, entering the living room. "Happy now?"

Matteo jumped into his arms, waving a square wooden box in the air. "Uncle Romeo, look what Ms. Zoe got me! It's an edible chemistry set," he said proudly, wearing a toothy smile. "I'm going to make rocks and fossils for everyone to eat for brunch!"

His family members laughed, then one by one turned toward the fireplace. That's when Romeo saw her. Zoe. For a moment, he thought he was dreaming, but as she crossed the room toward him, her floral perfume filled his nostrils and Romeo realized she wasn't a figment of his imagination. Beautiful in a sparkly tunic, black dress pants and ankle-tie pumps, he admired her effortless style. He wanted to kiss her, to wrap her up in his arms, but resisted the urge.

"Merry Christmas," she said, stopping in front of him. "It's good to see you."

His tongue was tied, but he managed to speak. "Zoe, what are you doing here?"

"You invited me to spend the holidays with you and your family, remember?"

"That was before we broke up. We're not together anymore. You shouldn't be here."

Francesca raised a hand in the air. "I picked her up an hour ago, and I'm glad I did. Zoe did nothing wrong."

Glancing around the living room, Romeo saw the sympathetic expressions on the faces of his family members and sighed heavily. Was he missing something? Why weren't his relatives on his side? Was he the only one who had a problem with what Zoe had done?

Shrieks, giggles and cheers erupted around the room as his nieces and nephews ripped wrapping paper to shreds, tossed it in the air as if it were confetti, then ran around in circles.

"Romeo, can we go somewhere quiet to talk?"

He shook his head, refused to consider her request. "Whatever you have to say to me you can say right here. What you did not only affected me, it affected my entire family, and they deserve to know the truth just as much as I do."

"Baby, I didn't do it. I swear. I love you, and I would never do anything to hurt you," she said, meeting his gaze. "You mean the world to me, and all I want is for you to be healthy and happy. I would never, ever do anything to jeopardize the incredible bond we have."

Romeo stared into her eyes. She'd said those words before, when they were arguing at the Wonderland Ball, but this time was different. Her voice was strong, convincing, the expression on her face one of fierce determination.

Romeo believed her. Sensed in his gut that she was telling the truth. But if she didn't betray him, then who did?

"I went to Casa Di Moda yesterday to resign, because I thought Aurora and Davide were behind the story, but I found Jiovanni in my office snooping through my things. I quickly put two and two together." Water filled her eyes, and her lips trembled.

"Go on. I'm listening."

"Jiovanni must have read my journal, photocopied the entries I wrote about our weekend at your villa, then gave them to his girlfriend, Alessandra. They paid someone to blackmail you, and when that didn't work they sold the information to the media. I never had anything to do with it…"

Joy, sadness and anger flooded his heart in equal measures. Disgusted by what Jiovanni had done, Romeo felt his eyes narrow and his hands curls into fists. Wasn't he supposed to be Zoe's best friend? How could he betray someone he claimed to love and respect? Romeo had never liked the associate designer and suspected he'd been plotting to break them up from day one. Thankfully, his evil scheme didn't work. "Jiovanni must have also tipped off the paparazzi about the Il Divo concert and the location of my villa as well," he said, thinking out loud. "That's how they knew where to find us."

"He must have, because I didn't tell a soul. We agreed to keep our relationship quiet, and since I was determined to keep my promise to you I had stopped confiding in Jiovanni about my personal life. I never imagined he'd snoop through my things though."

Hope surged through his body, filling his heart to the brim. A feeling of elation came over him, but Romeo didn't sweep Zoe into his arms and dance around the living room.

He wanted to hear everything, though, didn't want to miss anything she said.

"Baby, I'm so sorry about what Jiovanni did. I wish I could have stopped him, but—"

He interrupted her, couldn't stand to hear her apologize on Jiovanni's behalf, and pressed a finger to her mouth to stop her from saying another word. "Don't apologize for him. What happened is not your fault, it's his."

"I know, but I still feel horrible about it."

Romeo wore a sad smile. "And, I feel like an ass for the way I treated you."

"You do?" she asked, her eyes wide.

"Yes, I do. I jumped to conclusions instead of listening to your side of the story. I'm sorry. I was angry and upset after my run-in with that scumbag in the men's room and I lost my temper. I hope you can find it in your heart to forgive me."

"Of course, I forgive you. You're the man I love."

Zoe threw her arms around his neck and held him tight. Closing her eyes, she pressed her lips to his mouth. She kissed him slowly, tenderly, as if they had all the time in the world to please each other, and they did. Romeo wasn't going anywhere, would gladly spend the rest of the day making out with the woman he loved.

"I love you so much, and I can't live another day without you."

"Bellissima, you won't have to. I'm man enough to admit I made a mistake. I promise I'll never hurt you again or doubt your love. You have my word."

His family cheered as if they were watching a football game on TV, and Romeo laughed. "I missed you."

"I missed you, too," Zoe whispered, caressing the back of his head. "The last five days have been torture without you, and if not for Francesca, I never would have survived."

Romeo kissed the tip of her nose. "Bellissima, it sounds like you could use some R and R. How do you feel about spending New Year's Eve in Trinidad?"

"Trinidad? Really? Baby, that would be amazing!"

"You can say that again. We're going to have a blast on the island."

"I can see it now. Eating juicy mangoes, strolling along Mayaro Beach hand in hand, dirty dancing to calypso and soca music."

"Don't forget making love," Romeo added, caressing her cheeks with his thumb.

Closing her eyes, she gave him a sweet, soft kiss on the lips. "Can we leave tonight?"

"No," he whispered, against her mouth, "but when the coast is clear we can tiptoe upstairs for a Christmas Day quickie."

"Diavolo Sexy strikes again!" she joked. "Romeo, your family's here, and they have tons of activities planned this afternoon. We can't spend the rest of the day in bed—"

"Like hell we can't! My house, my rules, and *all* I want for Christmas is you."

Chuckling, Romeo sat down on his favorite chair, pulled Zoe down onto his lap, kissed her lips. The living room was crowded and noisy, filled with excitement as his family members sipped champagne and opened their presents. Romeo had everything he needed in Zoe, and didn't care what was under the tree. She was the center of his world, his one true love, and he'd never get tired of being with her. They shared the same hobbies and interests, and were a hundred percent committed to each other. Zoe understood him, appreciated him, and more than anything, made him feel loved and accepted. And it had nothing to do with his net worth.

Romeo took her hand to his, raised it to his mouth and

kissed her palm. In a playful mood, he couldn't resist teasing her and flashed a toothy smile. "I've lived a lot and experienced the best of everything, but you are the greatest thing that has ever happened to me, bellissima. Thanks for crashing your bike into my Lambo that fateful November morning."

"No, thank you," she insisted. An amused expression covered her face. "I can't take all of the credit. After all, *you* caused the accident, not me!"

Romeo gave an unrestrained laugh. His heart was full of love and happiness, and his smart, beautiful girlfriend was the reason why. Holding the woman he loved in his arms, surrounded by his relatives, was the best Christmas gift Romeo had ever received. He was in such a good mood he knew he'd never be able to wipe the smile off his face.

* * * * *

KIMANI™ ROMANCE

COMING NEXT MONTH
Available December 19, 2017

#553 PLAYING WITH SEDUCTION
Pleasure Cove • by Reese Ryan
Premier event promoter Wesley Adams is glad to be back in North
Carolina. Until he discovers the collaborator on his next venture is
competitive volleyball player Brianna "Bree" Evans, the beauty he spent
an unforgettable evening with more than a year ago. Will their past cost
them their second chance?

#554 IT'S ALWAYS BEEN YOU
The Jacksons of Ann Arbor • by Elle Wright
Best friends Dr. Lovely "Love" Washington and Dr. Drake Jackson wake
up in a Vegas hotel to discover not only did they become overnight
lovers, they're married. But neither remembers tying the knot. Will they
finally realize what's been in front of them all along—true love?

#555 OVERTIME FOR LOVE
Scoring for Love • by Synithia Williams
Between school, two jobs and caring for
her nephew, Angela Bouler is keeping it all
together...until Isaiah Reynolds bounces into
her life. Angela's hectic life doesn't quite mesh
with the basketball star's image of the perfect
partner. Winning her heart won't be easy, but
it's the only play that matters...

#556 SOARING ON LOVE
The Cardinal House • by Joy Avery
Tressa Washington will do anything to escape
the disastrous aftermath of her engagement
party. Even stow away in the back of
Roth Lexington's car and drive off with the
aerospace engineer. In his snowbound cabin,
they'll learn that to reach the heights of love,
they'll have to be willing to fall...

Get 2 Free Books,
<u>Plus</u> 2 Free Gifts—
just for trying the Reader Service!

KIMANI™ ROMANCE

YES! Please send me 2 FREE Harlequin® Kimani™ Romance novels and my 2 FREE gifts (gifts are worth about $10 retail). After receiving them, if I don't wish to receive any more books, I can return the shipping statement marked "cancel." If I don't cancel, I will receive 4 brand-new novels every month and be billed just $5.69 per book in the U.S. or $6.24 per book in Canada. That's a savings of at least 12% off the cover price. It's quite a bargain! Shipping and handling is just 50¢ per book in the U.S. and 75¢ per book in Canada.* I understand that accepting the 2 free books and gifts places me under no obligation to buy anything. I can always return a shipment and cancel at any time. The free books and gifts are mine to keep no matter what I decide.

168/368 XDN GLWV

Name	(PLEASE PRINT)

Address	Apt. #

City	State/Prov.	Zip/Postal Code

Signature (if under 18, a parent or guardian must sign)

Mail to the Reader Service:
IN U.S.A.: P.O. Box 1341, Buffalo, NY 14240-8531
IN CANADA: P.O. Box 603, Fort Erie, Ontario L2A 5X3

Want to try two free books from another line?
Call 1-800-873-8635 or visit www.ReaderService.com.

*Terms and prices subject to change without notice. Prices do not include applicable taxes. Sales tax applicable in NY. Canadian residents will be charged applicable taxes. Offer not valid in Quebec. This offer is limited to one order per household. Books received may not be as shown. Not valid for current subscribers to Harlequin® Kimani™ Romance books. All orders subject to approval. Credit or debit balances in a customer's account(s) may be offset by any other outstanding balance owed by or to the customer. Please allow 4 to 6 weeks for delivery. Offer available while quantities last.

Your Privacy—The Reader Service is committed to protecting your privacy. Our Privacy Policy is available online at www.ReaderService.com or upon request from the Reader Service.

We make a portion of our mailing list available to reputable third parties that offer products we believe may interest you. If you prefer that we not exchange your name with third parties, or if you wish to clarify or modify your communication preferences, please visit us at www.ReaderService.com/consumerschoice or write to us at Reader Service Preference Service, P.O. Box 9062, Buffalo, NY 14240-9062. Include your complete name and address.

KROM17R2

LOVE
Harlequin
romance?

Join our Harlequin community to share your thoughts and connect with other romance readers!

Be the first to find out about promotions, news, and exclusive content!

Sign up for the Harlequin e-newsletter and download a free book from any series at

www.TryHarlequin.com

CONNECT WITH US AT:

Harlequin.com/Community

Facebook.com/HarlequinBooks

Twitter.com/HarlequinBooks

Instagram.com/HarlequinBooks

Pinterest.com/HarlequinBooks

ReaderService.com

**ROMANCE WHEN
YOU NEED IT**

HSOCIAL2017

Want to give in to temptation with
steamy tales of irresistible desire?

Check out **Harlequin® Presents®,
Harlequin® Desire** and
Harlequin® Kimani™ Romance books!

New books available every month!

CONNECT WITH US AT:

Harlequin.com/Community

 Facebook.com/HarlequinBooks

Twitter.com/HarlequinBooks

Instagram.com/HarlequinBooks

Pinterest.com/HarlequinBooks

ReaderService.com

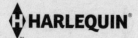

**ROMANCE WHEN
YOU NEED IT**

PGENRE2017